SERENDIPITY
FALLS

PATRICE WILTON

Other books by Patrice Wilton

REPLACING BARNIE
– book one in the Candy Bar series

WHERE WISHES COME TRUE
– book two in the Candy Bar series

NIGHT MUSIC
– book three in the Candy Bar series

REVENGE IS SWEET
– single title Women's Fiction

CHAMPAGNE FOR TWO
– single title Contemporary Romance

ALL OF ME
– single title Women's Fiction

A HERO LIES WITHIN
– Contemporary Romance

HANDLE WITH CARE
– Contemporary Romance

AT FIRST SIGHT
– Contemporary Romance

WEDDING FEVER
– book two in the SERENDIPITY FALLS series
Coming soon!

PROLOGUE

I'm Cupid. You know, that cute little angel floating around with a tiny bow and arrow. Well, let me tell you something-it's not so cute when you're 180 years old. Not in human life, but in Cupid life. We live to be at least 500, giving joy and love to humans who don't even believe we exist.

Not that I'm grumpy, but this sure is a thankless job. If you have a moment I'll tell you why.

I live in the small California town of Serendipity Falls. It's a popular tourist spot due to the spectacular 200-foot waterfall that streams down the side of the mountain and pools into an emerald green lake. It's the last place to fuel up, stretch your legs, or grab a bite to eat before you reach the ski hills at Mammoth. We're talking a gigantic mountain, with the highest elevation of any ski area around--over 11,000 feet, and if that doesn't scare you, nothing will.

I tried playing Cupid there because I like the cool mountain air, and I was fed up competing in "the big city" with Cupids younger than me, but that didn't work out. To be honest, I'm scared of heights, so I skedaddled, landing in this idyllic town. For all my grouching, I'm sure glad I did. The population is small so you'd think I'd get bored and move on, but that's not the case.

We have a brand spanking new mall that's attracting visitors to the area, with sporting good shops, snazzy boutiques and a slew of big name stores, like Wal-Mart, Home Depot, a Macy's, even Sears too. There's also a multiplex movie theatre, an ice-skating rink, and several restaurants to satisfy your appetite.

I have plenty of people to use as target practice with my arrows of love, but still, for all the zapping I do I never get any credit. That's my biggest beef with this place. The town folk boast about their falls and the natural spring water, and how romance blooms in Serendipity. I listen to them marvel about the unnatural amount of weddings, and I want to stamp my feet. Yes, I do have feet, pointy little ears, and a perfectly good bow and arrow, which I should use to pierce their backsides with. Perhaps, then I'd get some respect!

The only day I ever get recognition is Valentine's Day, and for me that's Christmas, Easter, every memorable holiday wrapped into one. I celebrate by binging on chocolate, and although I haven't met a truffle I didn't like, I'm especially partial to Godiva. Oh, dear, I got side-tracked, didn't I?

What I was saying is that in a town of ten thousand, we're having at least one wedding a month, and they think the water is responsible for that? Come on! I'm shooting pink darts, and I'm not so old that my aim's off either. I alternate my time between the mall and the restaurant across from the falls where I have the best view, the best leftover nibbles, and can see all the travelers who come through the door.

If you don't believe me, come by and see for yourself.

Oh, wait. Someone just walked in. A pretty young lady. She's alone and looks distraught. I better wander over and hear her story. You might want to listen in.

CHAPTER ONE

Tara Reynolds blasted through the door, drops of snow falling in clumps from her wool coat, scarf, and leather boots--suited more to city dwelling than mountain living.

She unwrapped the knitted scarf from the lower part of her face, then glanced at the mid-afternoon diners. A half dozen people sat in booths, and a lone man perched on a counter stool with his back to her. Place wasn't fancy, but had a homey feel, and smelled like baked bread and warm muffins just taken from the oven.

"Excuse me, but my car skidded off the road. Would anyone know of a number I could call for a tow?"

A couple of men glanced at each other and shrugged. "There's a garage down the road, but on Sunday's they're closed. One back in Bishop too." The guy who spoke looked from her to the rest of the people in the diner. "Anyone know if the Mammoth station's open?"

A plump waitress with blonde frizzy hair and pink glasses came forward. "Not sure, but if someone has one of those smart phones we could Google it."

Tara waved her iPhone in her gloved hand. "I can't get a connection. Must be the bad weather, right? You do get cell service up here, don't you?"

"Sure we do," the waitress answered. "This isn't the hicks, although our AT&T tower is not the most dependable service in the world. Swear it has PMS, it's so darn temperamental."

"Seriously? No open garage on a Sunday and a cell tower with female problems?" Tara's shoulders slumped and she gave a weary sigh. "Why did I agree to this? I'm not a survivalist or nature lover. I enjoy city lights, noise and traffic, crowded sidewalks, and all my creature comforts."

The waitress looked at her. "Have a nice cup of cocoa and a warm blueberry muffin, and I promise you things will look up."

"Sorry. Didn't mean to gripe. It's just that my car's in a ditch, and I'm supposed to meet someone in Mammoth in an hour. I'm renting a place for the winter, and the realtor is waiting for me."

"I can take you," a man said from a booth in the back.

Tara glanced his way but couldn't see him clearly. "That's nice of you to offer, but I can't accept." She bit her lip and sucked in a quick breath. Frustrated to the point of tears, she whispered, "I'm sorry, but I don't accept rides with strangers. Not in this day and age, that's for sure."

"That's smart. You shouldn't," he answered, stepping forward.

"Exactly." She removed her wool cap, sending a sprinkle of snow into the air. She shook out her hair and the copper curls fell to her shoulders. She needed to thaw out and the idea of hot chocolate and a warm muffin had her mouth watering. It wouldn't be the end of the world if she was a half hour late. "Is there a land-line I can use? I'll call a cab and leave the car until later."

The waitress nodded. "Sure there is, honey."

"Save your money and a good long wait," the man who'd offered the lift spoke again and stretched out his hand. "I'm Devon O'Reilley, and I live in Mammoth. Everyone there knows me."

Tara glanced around. "Does anyone here know this man?" At everyone's blank stare, she shook her head. "Nope. Nobody here can speak for you." She might be chilled to the bone, and late for an appointment, but common sense prevailed. "Thanks for the offer, just the same," she added with a friendly smile.

The smile turned to a grimace as she felt a sharp pang in the middle of her chest. "Ouch." She rubbed the sting, wondering if she'd strained herself with the hike up the snow-covered hill.

Devon stared at her, his hazelnut eyes darkening to a deep velvety chocolate, the kind that made you lick your fingers after you'd gobbled it up. He looked as if about to say something, then he turned around, paid his bill, and headed for the door instead. "Good luck then. Could be an hour or more before a cab arrives, or a tow."

He opened the door, and she hated to see him go. Icy air and snow flurries drifted in, making her rethink her decision. If she took the ride, she'd reach her appointment with time to spare. The roads were treacherous but he was sure to have a better equipped vehicle than a Mini.

She decided to ignore her mother's sage advice about not accepting rides with strangers, realizing if she delayed now she might not reach Mammoth at all tonight. The weather was setting in and looked to be a whopper of a storm. "Wait. I'll go with you, but first, can I see your driver's license?"

He shut the door so the cold air wouldn't blow through and removed his wallet from his back pocket. "You really don't trust people, do you?"

"It's a city thing," she answered with a shrug. He handed over the card, and she copied down the information before giving it back.

"Is that your current address?" she asked, glancing again at his ruggedly, handsome face.

"Yeah. Any other questions before we leave?"

"You're not a serial killer, are you?" She said it lightheartedly, almost as a joke, but her eyes met his with a challenge. After all, she'd watched enough TV to know that he fit the profile perfectly—attractive, intelligent, white, thirty-five.

"No." He gave a shrug with his big shoulders. "I haven't killed anyone lately, if that's what you want to know."

"Okay, then. Maybe I'm safe, and maybe I'm not. I have learned not to trust everything people say." She smiled to take any sting out of the words. "Big guy like you could snap me in two." In spite of herself she shivered, not the fearful kind, more like a delicious tingle.

His chiseled face looked carved from granite, fine-tuned by a master craftsman. Dreamy chocolate eyes skimmed over her. "You're safe enough."

She swallowed, and looked away. Staring at him was most unsettling. She either wanted to eat him or lick him all over--which was peculiar because she didn't have a sweet tooth.

"All righty, then." She gave his name and address to the waitress. "Could you keep this for me, and may I have your number too? That way, if you don't hear from me in an hour you can call the police."

"Sure, sweetie. My name's Sue Burke." She scribbled down her name and number and handed it to Tara. "Good luck to you both. Roads are getting worse by the minute."

Tara glanced at Devon and felt a pull at her heart. "Sue has your number, so if you have any weird thoughts of harming me, just head out the door."

His eyebrow shot up, and his granite face looked hotter than ever. "You coming?"

"I guess so." Tara sucked in a deep breath. Why couldn't he be forty and balding, instead of ruggedly handsome, tall, muscular, with a sexy cleft in his chin?

He might not be a pervert, but he was dangerous all right. Tara knew from first-hand experience that guys like him were better to steer away from. Hot guys weren't worth the pain. And yet, she had almost an irresistible urge to lick that cleft of his and see if his square jaw was as solid as it looked.

She jumped back, scared of her own thought. Where had that come from, and all the other weird notions in her head? Was the mountain air making her light headed, like a helium balloon at a rock concert?

"You all right?" he asked, his eyes narrowing. "You really scared of me?"

"No. I wouldn't agree to the ride, that being the case." What in the world was the matter with her? Her heart raced, and she felt a tightening low in her belly, a tingle that shouldn't be tingling, a sudden carnal need. Whoa— wait a damn minute! What the hell was going on?

She followed him out, noting his broad shoulders, tight jeans, and his great butt. She had to physically pry her eyes away and it was not a simple task. Matter-of-fact, she had to grit her teeth, close her eyes, and count to ten.

She must be more exhausted than she thought.

His jeep was out back, and she kept her eyes on the ground until they reached his vehicle. She hopped into the passenger seat, avoiding him entirely. "I appreciate this," she said in a private school, head-mistress kind of voice. "I'm sorry if I seemed ungrateful, but it's a scary world we're living in and a woman can't be too careful."

"Better to be safe than sorry," he replied and started the Jeep. "Fasten your seat belt. It could be a slippery ride. Some ice on the roads and the plows haven't had a chance to get here yet."

"I noticed that as I slid into the ditch." She did as instructed, and kept one hand next to the door handle, just in case.

He saw her hand and grinned. "You planning on jumping out?"

"Only if I have to." Feeling foolish, she released the door handle and clasped her hands in her lap. "How long do you think this storm will last?"

"Probably until tomorrow. You got anything in the car you might need tonight?"

"I have a suitcase, but I can get it later."

"There may not be a later."

"What do you mean?" Was that an ominous warning? If he planned to kill her-- which she highly doubted-- would he have his way with her first? She caught her breath as her heart pounded. Would he pounce quickly or take his time and do terrible, unmentionable things to her? She closed her eyes and envisioned him tearing at her clothes, his hard body covering hers as he pounded her into the snow-covered ground. Oh my! Only if there was a God in heaven.

His lip curled up. Had he read her thoughts?

Her pulse fluttered and she squeezed her knees together. This was ridiculous, she thought. Having erotic thoughts of being victimized--what was happening to her? She was a very normal, reserved, clever young woman. She never behaved inappropriately, not ever. Even when she went to senior prom and all the girls were sneaking drinks and losing their virginity in the backseats of cars, she'd remained sober and untouched.

He answered, "I only meant the roads will be impassable soon."

She sighed, not sure if that feeling inside her was disappointment. "Well, if you don't mind, perhaps we should stop."

"Where's your car?"

"Just down the road a bit, perhaps half a mile. I remember seeing a sign post welcoming us to Serendipity Falls. That was just before my car went into a skid."

He turned and headed south. The woods were very beautiful with the fallen snow--quiet, secluded, another world to the one she knew. With the snow falling so fast, the sky a dull grey, she wondered if she'd be able to spot her car.

"There it is!" she said with relief, and pointed to the Mini-Cooper nearly invisible with piled snow.

"You walked all that way?" he asked, sounding reluctantly impressed. "That was a tough hike."

"I work out." She added, "Besides, I had no choice."

"Need help with your bag?"

"Shouldn't think so." She returned a half second later. "I can't get the trunk open. It's stuck."

He jumped out and gave the trunk a good whack, but it still didn't budge. Going back to his Jeep, he retrieved a crowbar and pried it through the opening until the lock sprung free. Then he grabbed her bag and locked up the car.

"Damn thing's so small, it'll be good and buried by tomorrow." He glanced at her. "Is there anything here that can help you identify the spot?"

"Not sure." She thought for a sec. "What if we tied something around a branch in the tree?"

"We could try. Hand me your scarf."

She watched him shimmy a few feet up the tree and tie the red scarf on one of the lower branches. His long legs wrapped around the trunk, and she had a fleeting image of them wrapped around her.

She squirmed in the seat and forced herself to look away. What happened in that restaurant to make her thoughts so out of control? She was not the least bit promiscuous, but this Devon guy made her itch. If she were a dog she'd be humping his leg by now.

He returned to the car, got in, and headed back up the mountain. She was glad that he didn't feel the need to talk, as it was darn near impossible to look at him. Every time she did, she got a hot flash, and she wasn't even thirty yet.

He shifted his thigh and that was all it took. Rapidly, she fanned her face and closed her eyes, wondering if she was coming down with something.

"Are you all right? You're not going to be sick, are you?"

"No, I don't think so. I'm not sure. I feel heated. Maybe it's from that hike in the snow." She looked straight ahead. "Probably a head cold."

"Could be." He gave her a strange look. "You're perspiring and your color is bad. Should I pull over and let you out?"

"No. I'll be all right." She had to calm down. Being in the woods with this man was absolutely terrifying. The things she could do to him. The things he could do to her.

She breathed deeply, forcing herself to relax. She was moving, starting a new job, and now her car was in a ditch. Getting all worked up, it could happen to anyone. "So what do you do in Mammoth, Devon?"

"I run a bar," he answered without further elaboration.

"In the town or on the mountain?"

"In town." He gave her a quick glance. "What about you?"

"I'm a pastry chef at Cascade Resorts. I'll be working at the Grande. You want something sweet, you should come in sometime." When he didn't respond, she added, "I worked at the Cascade in Vegas for a year, then in Beverly Hills, now I've been transferred here."

"Sounds like a lot of moving around," he muttered.

"It's pretty standard in this business, especially if you want to keep climbing the ladder. Besides, I have nothing holding me back, and I enjoy new challenges." She'd had her heart broken again, by loser number three. Guy had turned out to be married, a secret he'd forgotten to share. Just another reason out of so many that she didn't trust the stuff men say. And a reason to focus on her career, not romance.

He fiddled with his radio dial and found a local station giving an update on the storm. She waited for the report to finish then asked, "And you? How did you end up here?"

"The mountain and me go way back."

She couldn't make anything of that, so she dug a little harder. "Do you have a family? Any little O'Reilley's running around town?"

"Not that I know of." She noticed a dimple in his cheek as he hid his smile.

Five minutes went by without either speaking a word, and mile by silent mile, she became more comfortable. "My fever has gone," she told him. "I can breathe again."

"Good. You had me worried."

"Must be an altitude thing." She dared a quick look at him, and was glad that her temperature didn't soar. "So you run a bar. What else do you do? You gotta ski, right?"

His jaw tightened. "I ski some."

"That's it? Some? I can't imagine why anyone would live in a ski town unless you were a ski bum." She laughed. "Can't be the weather."

He didn't answer, but his hands were tightly clenched on the wheel.

"Do you mind me asking you questions?"

"I moved to the mountains for quiet." He turned the radio back on and she took the hint.

"Fine. Not another word." She folded her arms and glanced out the side window. It was so beautiful up here, and after all the earlier exertion and stress, she began to relax. She rested her head back and found herself getting sleepy.

When they reached Mammoth, he asked where she wanted dropped off.

She yawned. "I'm meeting an agent from Admiral Realty. The office is in the village, that's all I know." She rummaged through her bag. "I have the phone number right here, but since my cell doesn't work, it won't do me much good."

"Try it. We're at a higher attitude and we get better reception here."

She did try it and it worked. "Cool." She called the realtor, then the waitress at Serendipity Falls. "Hi Sue. It's Tara, and I'm calling to say I arrived safe and sound."

"Good," she answered. "I hear the weather is getting worse."

"Thanks for looking out for me."

"Enjoy your stay here, and drop in the next time you're in town."

"I'll do that. Bye, Sue."

Tara looked around the tree-lined streets now heavily coated with snow, at the fairy lights overhead, and at the pretty storefronts. She smiled when she spotted a group of girls trying to capture the soft snow with their tongue as it fell on their uplifted faces. "This is a sweet town. I'm going to like it here."

"You say that now, but wait until busy season when the place is over run with high school and college kids out to party. Not to mention all the families and their pack of brats."

"You don't like young people?" She darted a quick look at him. He certainly was a sour grapes kind of guy. No wonder he wasn't married. Too moody.

"Not the unruly ones. Guess that comes with the territory of owning a bar."

"Well, I'm sure I'll be very happy working for the Grande." He stopped in front of the real estate office, and she jumped out of the Jeep. "Thanks for the ride and getting me here in one piece." She grinned. "Not that I expected to be chopped up or anything."

"Why do you think I wanted the suitcase?" he said with a low chuckle. "You need help getting it out of the back?"

"Nope. I'm good. So what's the name of the bar? Maybe I'll stop in and say 'hi'."

"It's an Irish pub called The Cock and Bull."

"Sounds lovely." She stood with her bag in her hands and gave him a mock salute. "Tally-ho. Hope the storm doesn't keep your rowdy customers away."

"I could use a quiet night." He nodded at her. "See you around town." He took off and she walked into the realtor office.

"I'm Tara Reynolds," she told the receptionist, "and I'm here to see Ken Johnson."

"That's me." A lean, clean-cut, young man around thirty left his desk and came to shake her hand. "Glad you made it up here in this storm. Did you have any trouble?"

"My car's parked in a ditch near Serendipity Falls, but someone offered me a ride."

"That was decent of him. Who is it? I know most of the locals around here."

"Devon O'Reilley. He runs a bar in town."

Ken's eyes darkened and the smile left his face. "That son-of-a-bitch? Excuse me, I shouldn't speak like that to a client, but he's not one of my favorite people." He rubbed his jaw. "You're lucky you got here in one piece."

CHAPTER TWO

"What do you mean?" Tara stammered. "I must admit I was concerned about accepting a ride with a stranger, but here I am."

"Let's just say, he's got a reputation with pretty women." Ken shook his head with a look of disgust.

"Oh." For a second, she felt disappointed. Obviously, he had not found her the least bit attractive. "Guess I wasn't his type."

"Lucky for you." Ken gave her a once over. "Since you're new in town, I'll give you a warning. Stay clear of him. He's trouble with a capital T."

She wondered what Devon had done to cause this much animosity. She had certainly not found anything to fault him. Although not overly talkative, he'd been pleasant enough, and gone out of his way for her—a complete stranger.

"So, you must be anxious to see this new place you've rented," Ken said, obviously wanting to change the subject. "The location is ideal, and it should be very comfortable." He grabbed keys, and headed for the door.

"It's close enough to town that we could walk, but not in this weather."

"If it's as nice as the online photos, I'm sure it's a gem."

Her suitcase was quite large and the wheels didn't work well in the snow, but Ken handled it with ease and she followed him to his car. Once they were settled he drove out of the village to a residential area a few blocks away. "Near enough to the action," he said, "but just outside the noise."

"It's perfect," she said, smiling with delight. The A-frame cottage was adorable with red painted window shutters, a full porch, a couple of rocking chairs, and a covered pile of wood near the door.

"I'll show you around and get the fire started before I leave," he offered.

"That's very kind of you." She had to admit the people she had encountered so far were much friendlier than city folk. Everyone in L.A. was either too busy making money or making headlines to be nice.

Ken unlocked the door and brought her bag in, then turned on the lights. It was comfortably furnished with two large, plush sofas and a wooden, square table in the middle. One of the honey colored sofas faced a brick wall with a huge fireplace and the other faced a large, fifty-inch TV. Two more comfy chairs sat underneath a window, with an ottoman and a small, round table. It seemed like the perfect place to curl up and read a book.

"This is great. More spacious than I thought it would be."

"It's only fourteen hundred square feet. Two bedrooms in the loft, separated by a full bath. As you'll see, not an inch of space goes to waste."

"I love it already." She meandered into the kitchen while Ken brought in the firewood and started the fire.

"You know how to do this?" he asked.

"I'm pretty sure I can handle it. My dad took me camping as a kid. It's been awhile though." She watched the fire as memories stirred. Her mother hated camping, but went along with it because she and her Dad had enjoyed the whole earthy experience of pitching a tent, sleeping on air mattresses, and roasting wieners and marshmallows in the camp fire. "Did you use kindling or a presto log to get things going?"

"The log is quicker," he said, "and easier." He gave her an easy-going smile that made his eyes crinkle and two small dimples appear.

"I'm all for that." She walked back into the living room. "Would you mind if I ride with you back into town? I need to pick up a few things and make arrangements for my car."

"Of course–anything you need to get settled in, I'll be glad to help."

He dropped her off at a market and told her he'd go back to his office and arrange a tow. "Call me when you're done, and I'll drive you back home." Ken was just the right amount of friendly and didn't stir a single sexy thought. No need to be on guard with him.

"I appreciate that," she answered with a happy smile.

She grabbed a cart and wandered up and down the aisles, choosing fresh produce, meats, and necessary staples, tossing in some unhealthy snacks and a few bottles of good wine as well. Why not? This had been the most auspicious beginning to her new life here. It started out so dismally when her car skidded off the road, but because of that, she'd discovered the beauty of living in a small town.

Two strangers had gone out of the way to help her. She must somehow find a way to repay them for their kindness. Perhaps she could invite them over for dinner—not together, of course, obviously there was some bad blood between them.

Must be a woman, she decided, what else would cause such friction between two men? Ken was a likeable, outgoing kind of guy, but Devon was intriguing. The strong, silent type, or just secretive? If he was hiding something from his past, she'd love to know what.

She paid for her groceries and called Ken to say she'd wait for him outside.

"It's freezing. Wait near the door and I'll swing by."

Normally, Tara would have complied, but she was dressed warm and had a curiosity about the town. She took the cart and waited in front of the market, then after a few minutes, she headed up the street. Was that a Cock & Bull sign on the other side of the road?

She wished she could walk over to find out, but she had to return the shopping cart. Devon must have thought she was incredibly weird, with her questions and her hot flushes. What had caused them, she wondered? Had it been stress? If so, what about all those erotic, crazy thoughts? How freakin' bizarre was that? So unlike her. She was a perfectly sane woman most of the time.

Just as well that she didn't check out his bar tonight. Whatever she'd been experiencing, she wanted it gone, never to resurface. They would both be living in this town, and even having those thoughts privately was embarrassing.

Quickly, she retraced her steps and arrived back at the market just as Ken pulled up. He jumped out and helped her with the bags, and insisted on unloading them at her cabin.

She'd noticed Ken was easy on the eye back at the realtor's office. Not traditionally handsome, but appealing in a boyish, charming kind of way. The kind of guy that could grow on you—if you let him. He had light brown hair that was thinning on top, bright blue eyes, and a very nice smile with white even teeth. Safe, pleasant, maybe even slightly boring. Certainly not dangerous. She'd bet a week's wage that he didn't have a bad-ass bone in his body.

She waited until the important things were sorted and put away, then offered him a glass of wine. He walked over to the fireplace and tossed in another log. "Sounds good, and then I'll leave and let you settle in. You've had a busy day," he observed pleasantly.

She poured the wine and handed him a glass. They sat on the sofa to watch the fire. Unlike Devon, he didn't set off any hot flashes or wicked thoughts, so she felt quite comfortable sharing a drink in her new home. "Thank you so much for all your help. Did you have any luck with the car?"

"The local garages were shut today, so I called AAA. They said they should have it to you within the next couple of hours." He folded his legs, staring into the fire. "By tomorrow morning the car would likely be buried."

"I know. I'm so grateful that you rescued it for me."

"No big deal. Least I could do after your bad start here."

"Not such a bad start. You've been very kind to me." She darted a quick look at him but he seemed more interested in the fire. "I guess I should join AAA, but I never had a reason to before. When I lived in LA, I rarely drove. The traffic was horrendous, so I mainly used public transport."

"Well, you're going to need your own car up here. And you may want to consider trading in your Mini for a four-wheeler."

"I love my little car, and I only bought it a few years ago." She frowned. "I'm certainly not buying a truck or a family SUV."

"Just saying." He glanced out the window. "The snow's rough but mudslides in the spring can be equally as dangerous."

"I know you're right, but it's unlikely that I'll be staying long enough to make it worthwhile. The Cascade resort has me moving around a lot." She sipped from her wine then put the glass down. "Isn't this kind of early for a snowstorm? It's only the first week of November."

"It happens that way sometimes. We're hit early and then it settles down. Good for the mountain and the skiers, bad for commuters."

"Can't imagine people commuting. Where would they commute from?"

"There are a few small towns in the area, and an airport. A lot of people work here and live locally, and every weekend we have a steady stream of traffic from San Francisco and LA."

"Tell me more. How many people live here year round? What do people do for excitement?"

"There's plenty to do, winter and summer. We have around 8500 living in Mammoth Lakes, and a lot of tourists that come for summer vacations or winter skiing." He uncrossed his legs and seemed to relax, as though talking about his favorite subject. "We have our natural hot springs, pristine streams and lakes for fishing, hiking and cross country trails. There are golf courses and summer festivals, shopping and restaurants. Something for everyone." He grinned. "If you can't be happy here, you can't be happy anywhere."

Tara laughed. "Is that your real estate slogan?"

"No," Ken answered. "But it should be."

She had a big sip of wine then blurted, "Why do you dislike Devon so much? He was very nice to me. A perfect gentleman."

Ken shifted his weight and put his glass on the table. "Don't let that fool you. He takes what he wants and doesn't think twice. The guy uses women the way some men use power. They figure it's their due."

"I don't know him, but he didn't strike me like that."

"Ask my sister. She came up here for ten days last Christmas and he romanced her big time. When she left, he never called again, just dropped her and moved on." He finished his wine, got up, and put the glass on the kitchen counter. "She's still heart-broken. She's only twenty-three."

"Really?" She stood too. "You're right. That does make him sound like a jerk."

He nodded. "Well, now you know. He doesn't seem to have anything to do with the local girls, only the ones from the city who come here on weekends." He gave her a speculative look. "He takes his relationships casual, a quick tumble then he's in and out. But I don't think you need to worry. He won't bother you."

What the heck did that mean? Did he find her unattractive too? She ran a hand through her still damp hair that had been snowed upon, and flattened by a snug wool cap, and licked her dry, chapped lips. Not that she cared what Devon and Ken thought of her, but damn, she must look a fright.

She patted her face, noticing how dry and rough the skin felt after only a few hours in the frigid mountain air. Yikes! She was visually aging by the minute--which was just as well. At least she wouldn't experience heartbreak here. "I'll make sure he won't. Or anyone else. I'm only passing through." She walked Ken to the door. "Thanks again for your help today."

"Enjoy your new home. Call me if you need anything."

"I'll do that."

Shortly after Ken left, a tow truck arrived with her car. The driver had also found her scarf and returned it to her. She thanked him profusely and gave him a big tip, then put the scarf around her neck, and tugged on her boots. Going outside, she moved her Mini under the covered carport, then returned indoors.

She had a light dinner, too tired to do more. After she'd cleaned up, she sat down in the cozy chair near the window to read a new book. She must have fallen asleep for when she awoke the embers had burned out, and the night was dark. She turned off all the lights except the lamp near the reading chair, then climbed the stairs, claimed the larger bedroom as her own, and crawled in bed. It had been an exhausting day, and tomorrow, she'd begin her first day on her new job.

She put her head on the feathered pillow and closed her eyes. Images of the playboy Devon came to mind. He had devilish good looks; long, curly, dark hair; sparkling deep brown eyes; a killer body, and a moody disposition. Lucky for her, he only liked the city girls because she didn't want anything to do with him.

The guy didn't even like kids. Probably kicked puppies too, she decided, flipping over to her side. It was extremely unfortunate that he had this magnetic sex appeal, because she always seemed to be attracted to the wrong kind of guys. Guys with a wicked gleam in their eyes, and a will too strong to resist. The very kind her dear, sweet mom had warned her about. Wasn't it time for a new beginning? After all, she'd had her share of men like that, and three in one lifetime was three too many.

She'd come to the mountains to forget her last big mistake, and to keep moving forward, her eyes on the prize. A relationship was the last thing she needed. A good lay once in awhile would be agreeable. Sex, no strings attached. After all, she didn't want to put roots down anywhere. She preferred being flexible, not strapped down to one place or one person.

But damn. Too bad that Devon didn't date local girls, because man-oh-man, he was hot!

CUPID

Sheesh! I'd jumped into her scarf when she left the restaurant, and then Mister Big and Tall hung me in the tree. Luckily for me, I'd been able to jump down and land on the suitcase he'd gotten out of her car. I'd had to ride in the back of the jeep all the way up the mountain, and it had been a jiggly, bumpy ride, for sure. Still, it beat spending the night dangling from a tree on a cold, blistery night. If I'd attempted to wing my way up the mountain, my delicate flappers would have turned into icicles before that first mile.

The evening turned out well, all things considered. I spent a nice night cozied up in front of the fire, and enjoyed a cup of hot chocolate, with marshmallows too. While sipping on my sinfully good drink--sinfully, because I'd spiked it with a hair of brandy--I'd flashed back to the drive up the mountain and the spirited conversation between the two new lovebirds. All those hot flashes had been my doing, of course. And her naughty thoughts—oh, what fun! If only I could get some credit once in a while, it would make my life's work more fulfilling, but I mustn't complain. I'm an excellent Cupid and use only the very best specimens, good people who don't know what their life is missing until I show them how much more enjoyable it is with the right companion. Unlike some Cupids I know, who will remain nameless, I take an active interest in the falling-in-love process and help guide the couple along. Some are more stubborn than others and need a good nudge once in a while. I stay until I know they can make it on their own.

Bringing love and joy to the humans always makes me a little sad too, for there's no happy ending for me. I'm doomed to travel life alone, for that's a Cupid's fate, and I really should accept it with good grace.

The only problem is-- I'm in love with love.

CHAPTER THREE

Devon rubbed his backside. He had a pang that reminded him of sciatica, and he knew from experience how that injury could linger. Would put a kibosh on his skiing too. He couldn't remember doing anything to cause the pinched nerve, which twanged every time he used his left hip. He'd reached into his back pocket to pull out his driver's license when that girl at the restaurant had demanded it, and a second later, he'd felt a sharp stab. It hadn't lasted long. Nothing that should cause this lingering, annoying discomfort.

Better not keep him away from the ski hills—the snow should be outstanding tomorrow morning, and he couldn't wait to make some fresh tracks. Skiing was the only time he could outrace his thoughts.

"Hey, Kyle," Devon said, watching his younger brother hang freshly washed glasses over the bar. "We might as well close up early. Nobody's going to come out in this storm."

Kyle nodded. "You're probably right. It's been a ghost town since quarter after nine."

"You ready to wrap it up?" Devon remained seated, enjoying a beer as Kyle busied himself cleaning, counting the cash, doing all the menial tasks that he didn't seem to mind.

Three years ago, next month to be exact, they had lost their grandparents in a tragic accident, while they were celebrating their fiftieth anniversary in the Greek Isle of Santorini. Two buses met on a curve and neither gave way, and the consequences were deadly. There had been a class action suit, and the named beneficiaries in their will had received a loss of life settlement just under two million dollars. With their share, Devon and Kyle had bought this business. It was fine during the ski season, but the summers were slow and with the high rent they were barely scratching out a living. Still, living here, year round, made things bearable.

Their sister, Mila, on the other hand, had turned her little business venture into gold. She owned a boutique in the Serendipity Mall, called Wedding Fever, which sold consignment wedding dresses, wedding favors and gifts, twenty-four hour service on invitations, and a two-day special order on wedding cakes. Everything a spur of the moment bride and groom could need for a fast weekend wedding--and gourmet aphrodisiacs for the hopeful guests attending. Being one step ahead of the game, she'd seen the wedding frenzy going on and taken it to the bank. Proudly, she'd tell people she wasn't a romanticist, but a capitalist.

The two brothers should have taken her advice and opened up a wedding chapel instead of a bar. They would be rolling in dough instead of rolling in debt. Still, the

Cock and Bull was their pride and joy—and major source of headache.

Kyle and Devon, three years apart, were different in many ways, but they both loved skiing, extreme sports, hot women, and this bar.

"You want a beer?" he asked Kyle.

"Naw. I'm good." Kyle placed the cash in a locked safe, leaving only small bills in the till. "You went to the bank in Serendipity today. How did that go?"

"They agreed to a low interest loan for six months. We should be able to pay it off after the winter season."

"That's good then. The summer's always flat, you know that." Kyle glanced out the window. "This snowfall will help."

"It will. Especially if we can get a few days of it." He grinned, and toasted the weather with his pint of ale. "Bring on the snow." He took a slug, and shifted his weight on the stool.

Devon was the worrier in the family. He didn't like living hand to mouth, especially with the economy so damn bad. They had used most of their money to buy the business, but the rent was killing them. Perhaps it would have been wiser to get something off the main street, but that was hindsight. Their parents had run a small lodge in Napa Valley for years and had sold it after the grandparent's ill-fated trip to retire in Maui. As youngsters, Devon and his siblings had seen how hard it was to make ends meet in a tourist oriented business, but that hadn't deterred any one of them. Running a business, headaches and all, was a normal way of life.

Lately the news was filled with doom and gloom. Europe's economy was in the sewer, this country was going down the tube. Hell, the world was falling apart and nothing was safe anymore. If he'd been smart, he would have bought a business in Alaska. Nobody cared enough to blow it to smithereens.

He rubbed his backside again. "I hope I can ski tomorrow. It's going to be dream conditions, but I've got a shooting pain right here."

"You're always a pain in the butt," Kyle said with a grin. "You know that."

"And you're always carefree." He cuffed the back of his brother's head and knuckled his unruly curls. "So how's Lisa? Did you guys get together today?"

"She was working until three, but I took her for a late lunch before coming over here." Kyle slipped out from under the bar. "It's still early yet. Maybe I'll take a run over to her place and see if she's up."

"Might as well. I'm heading home. See you when you show up." Devon slid off the bar seat and stretched. "Don't do anything I wouldn't do."

"No chance of that. We all know you'd do anything."

Devon made a wounded face. "Why does everyone think that? I'm just a regular guy."

"Like hell. From the time you made the Olympic team, you've been the glamour boy with the bad rep." Kyle grinned. "How come you're not shacking up with some sweet thing?"

"Not interested. Running the bar is enough trouble, without some hot babe complicating my life." He ran a hand over his chin. "Besides, I'm not all that sociable anymore. Prefer my alone time."

"That sucks, you ask me. What you need is to get laid regularly. Find a steady girl instead of a stream of one nighters."

"No, thanks. I've got it made, man. I can date when I please, and don't have to be around someone when I don't want to be."

"Heed my warning," Kyle said. "You're getting older every day. Your babe-magnet days are numbered."

Devon punched Kyle in the arm. "Go have fun with Lisa. If you need any help, give me a call."

"As if." Whistling, Kyle dangled his car keys and headed for the door. "You coming or staying to lock up?"

"I'm coming." He limped toward the door. "Damn leg. The cold makes the arthritis in my knee act up."

Kyle snickered. "See—told you. Arthritis, sciatica, what will it be next? A hair piece?"

"My hair isn't a mop like yours, but I'm not losing it either." As if checking, he ran a hand through the mess. "I should have had a cut when I was in town, but with the weather so bad, I decided to get moving. Besides, a woman needed a ride. Her car skidded off the road and ended in the ditch."

"Since when did you become the good Samaritan?" Kyle glanced at his brother's face. "Oh, she was a looker. Right?"

"I didn't say that."

"You didn't have to. Hey, you're blushing. Shit. What's with that?" He laughed. "Oh, man. Don't tell me. The love bug got you, didn't it?" He hooted, doubling over.

"That's rich. You know what they say about Serendipity. It's the spring water. Did you drink some?"

"I had a bottle while I was waiting for the banker." Devon rubbed his jaw. "That's hog-wash anyway. Just an old wife's tale."

"That's what you say now, but wait until that bug works its way into your system." He smirked. "Hope you have some money saved up, because you're going to need it."

"What the hell are you going on about?" Devon could feel his Irish temper flare. "If I had money, I wouldn't be asking bankers for a loan."

"That's true. But I wasn't thinking about the bar." Kyle grinned. "Figured with you smitten, you might need extra cash for a wedding."

"You're starting to tick me off. Shut up about it, will you?"

"No need to get hostile, bro, but you have to admit, a wedding a month in that small of a town is a little crazy, right? The population is only ten thousand; that's a lot of love-making going on." He whistled. "You might want to schedule yours soon before all the best places are booked."

"One more word out of you, and I'll put my fist in your mouth." Devon glared at his kid brother. "I'm not getting married. I'm having too good a time, just as it is."

"You should have thought about that earlier. Hell, I stay as far away from Serendipity and that spring water as I can. I'm only twenty-eight. I don't want bitten by no love bug."

"What about Lisa?" Devon demanded, feeling a stream of heat emanating from his body. "You've already got it bad."

"No, I've got it good." Kyle eyed his brother. "You're sweating. You better go home and rest." He laughed. "Save your energy for that wedding night."

"Very funny." Devon jumped into his Jeep and started the motor. "Give Lisa my love, unless you'd rather I did it myself." He grinned when his brother flipped him the bird.

At least that shut him up.

He fiddled with the heater as he drove the short distance back to the cabin he shared with Kyle. It was on a lake, and in the summer they had a small boat they used for fishing and water-skiing. They each had a jet ski too. He sure couldn't complain about his life. He loved the mountain living, all year round. The city was close enough when he got the urge. Not that he got it very darn often.

He sneezed, and felt a chill run over him. Maybe that girl, Tara, transferred her fever to him. Just his luck. He'd gone out of his way to help her, and now he might be laid up in bed instead of *swooshing* down the mountain in the fresh virgin snow.

The word virgin stuck in his head, for that's exactly what she looked like. There had been an innocence about her--she'd looked fresh. Excited about life in general. Hopes, dreams. Ambition. Unlike him, who knew that his best years had already come and gone.

Perhaps he was jaded, but he had good reason to be. His grandparents had died so tragically, only in their mid-seventies. They'd been very active, loved boating and golf, and weekend getaways. The Mediterranean cruise had been a life-time dream. He knew about stuff like that.

His dream had been shattered too on a practice run in Turin. He'd flipped head over heels and barreled down the icy slope, coming to a bad end when he hit one of the bottom poles during the 2006 winter Olympics. Once he'd been stabilized, he was transferred from Turin, Italy to a big city hospital and rehab center where he'd spent darn near a year of his life. He'd sustained a serious head injury, which not too many people knew about. Had to practically relearn everything from square one.

Then when his mental skills strengthened, he had physical problems to deal with. The doctors doubted he'd ever ski again, when that was all he'd lived for from the time he was a kid. He'd busted his ass to make it to the Olympics. He hadn't minded giving up his carefree teenage years to focus on this one dream, working and training every single day. He'd done it without complaint, and then in an instant, everything he'd worked for was gone.

Steel pins held his leg together, but at least it got him up and down the slopes and his life wasn't over. Every blessed day he could be on top of the mountain, breathe that clear, fresh air, and see the glorious vista below him.

Damn, most days he considered himself the luckiest sonofabitch in the world. No way would he sell the business and move away from here. This was his home, the only place he knew, loved, and felt a measure of peace.

The cabin was dark when he entered. He ran into a chair, hit his bummed leg, and cursed God in heaven. He sat down to take his boots off and the pain in his ass hurt like a bitch.

He sucked in a breath and shivered, in spite of the fact his body burned with fever. He undressed and climbed into his large bed, bringing the down comforter up to his chin. His body ached, and his heart hammered.

Today would be the last damn time he'd drink that spring water in the valley. Whatever was in it, he didn't need to find out. He'd stick to Aquafina instead.

CHAPTER FOUR

Tara climbed out of bed and peeped out the window. The sun was shining, the snow that covered the roads and bushes seemed unnaturally bright, and the tree branches glistened. It was a beautiful sight.

She stretched her arms above her head, feeling glorious after her long sleep. Throwing a thick, fuzzy robe around herself, she padded to the kitchen to put on the coffee then settled into one of the comfy chairs near the window to look at the heavy drifts of snow. Looked like two feet in some spots. Deeper in other areas. Driving might be tricky, but she didn't have far to go.

The Grande Cascade Hotel and Spa was only a half mile down the street and that was one of the many reasons she'd chosen this cabin to rent. Figured she could walk if the roads weren't fit to drive.

She poured her coffee, made toast, and took both to her favorite chair by the window; once again, marveling at the dramatic new sights awaiting her. From this corner of the room, she could clearly see the mountain and the abundance of trails carved into the sides. She could make out the lifts and see a few wooden buildings as well.

Although she'd never lived in the mountains before, she had spent a few weekends with friends at Catamount in the Berkshires while attending culinary school in New York. But those mountains were like tiny foothills compared to the high Sierra in northern California. She was thankful she'd learned to ski, although she could only be classified as an intermediate skier at best. She preferred groomed slopes to the big moguls and more challenging runs.

Compared to living in the desert of Vegas and the parking lot of downtown L.A., all this open space and fresh air seemed very peaceful, a welcome respite from the noise, confusion and excitement that she normally loved. This would be like an extended vacation from the real world, and she'd enjoy it for as long as she could before the restless urge resurfaced, and she needed to move on. Usually, it was a man who drove her away, but not always. She'd had itchy feet ever since her mother died and that had been thirteen long years ago.

As a teenager, she'd watched her mother struggle with breast cancer for years. At times, she'd seem to get better and everyone would be full of hope, then the disease would come back and attack again. Tara had taken over the cooking in the house and had particularly enjoyed baking for her family, especially her mother. She'd decorate cupcakes or make a raspberry mousse, something pretty that they could share together when she got home from school. Then, one day, her mother's fight was over, and she wasn't there anymore.

Her mother had encouraged her to become a doctor. But after watching her mother slowly eaten away, the sight and the smell of a hospital bed, the treatments and the pain and suffering, she couldn't imagine that in her future. Creating beautiful desserts and seeing someone's face light up as they tasted it—that's what made her happy.

She loved her job, she loved her life, and if sometimes she was lonely, well that was her choice. If in the future she longed for more, she'd do something about it. Meanwhile, her only responsibility was to herself, and she liked that.

Tara showered, then dressed in a sweater and slacks, put on her boots and a hooded wool jacket, and grabbed her mitts. She drove the few blocks to the Grande Hotel, excited to meet the head executive chef and the rest of the culinary staff. She'd interviewed here in the spring but had to wait for an opening. She received the call for the job only two weeks ago.

She parked in the employee lot and, head high and arms swinging, she waltzed through the door, greeting everyone with a friendly smile.

Today was a new beginning. She liked new beginnings; they were so full of possibilities. Maybe she'd even be able to put her roots down here. Ken had certainly sung its praises, and the people did seem more genuine and caring than in a big city. It would be so nice to make friends and keep them. The transient life had chosen her, but sometimes, she felt she hadn't chosen it.

Marc Florien, the executive chef, welcomed her and introduced her to the rest of the culinary staff. "As most of you know, Tara Reynolds is joining our team as executive pastry chef, and from what I hear, we're lucky to have her." He gave her a warm smile. "She's worked for Cascade Resorts for five years, both in Las Vegas and Beverley Hills, and before that, she was with the Marriot. She's well trained, highly regarded, and should be a great addition to our staff."

The executive sous chef shook her hand. "I'm Phillip Simone, welcome aboard."

Everyone lined up to greet her, from the executives to the lowly dishwashers, and she made a mental note to remember everyone's name and connect with them on some personal level.

The first day on the job was like being tossed from the frying pan into the fire.

The hotel had a solar energy convention going on, and she needed to cater to two hundred for lunch, as well as afternoon tea, followed by dinner. Nothing could have made her happier. Throwing herself into her work, she organized the pastry staff, giving everyone detailed instructions, and had the kitchen happily humming in no time.

Marc Florian made it as easy as possible, having selected the menu, and all she had to do was follow it, but Tara felt the need to put her own mark on the desserts and added an extra flare. For the luncheon buffet, not only did they have the peach cobbler and strawberry torte, but platters of German chocolate truffles.

A variety of cookies were on the menu for the afternoon tea, but Tara ordered delicate mini cannolis as well. For the dinner dessert, they served raspberry cheesecake with chocolate ganache and a dazzling selection of luscious tarts and moussed mini's.

She didn't expect thanks for the extra work she heaped on her staff, but she had wanted to please the executive chef with her creativity and passion, plus make a good impression on the conference attendees.

At the end of the day, she was taking off her apron and getting ready to call it quits when the executive sous chef pulled her aside, his firm hand on her arm. "What the hell did you think you were doing?" he whispered in a low voice.

"I beg your pardon?" Tara disengaged his hand. "What's the matter, Philippe?"

"Come to my office. I need a word." Once inside, he closed the door, effectively trapping her. "This was your first day, and instead of following the catering selected by me and the event planner, you decided to go commando. You blew the budget and have half the staff complaining."

"I'm sorry, maybe I did go over the top, but I wanted to make a good impression." Tara straightened her shoulders and looked into the young man's face. "I'm good at what I do, and I have a reputation to protect. I don't want it compromised by mediocrity."

His eyes narrowed. "How did a little snip like you get such a high opinion of yourself? We are a team here, and I would thank you to remember that."

"I'm sorry, but when I stepped into the kitchen, I took over the reins. I love what I do, and my intent was not to make enemies, only to do the best job possible."

"In the future, stay with the plans and don't change them without discussing it with me." He opened the door and indicated that she could leave. "You came highly recommended, but no one person is bigger than the whole. Remember that."

"Of course. It's just...I can't explain it, but I don't want anything to be ordinary." Tara felt a warm flush fan over her neck and face. She should not have to apologize for being exceptional. That's why they'd hired her. "The delicacies are not only delicious they make people feel good--if only for a moment. That's important to me."

"Control your impulses or you'll be fired. There are twenty more applicants ready to take this job." Humiliated, she nodded and left in a hurry, hoping to escape before anyone saw her. She was about to push through the revolving door when Cindy, one of the assistants chefs, caught up with her.

"Tara! I just want to tell you that you were amazing. It was so much fun working with you today."

Tara looked at the girl, giving her a cautious smile—the compliment after the ass chewing acted as a balm to her wounded ego. "Really? I didn't work you too hard? I did get a little over excited today."

Cindy laughed. "Excited is a good thing, isn't it? We want to be inspired and you certainly gave us that."

"Thank you." The two women walked out, and Tara was immediately hit by the frigid air. She snuggled deeper into her wool coat and pulled on her gloves. "I may have overstepped myself today. Tomorrow, I promised Philippe that I'd stick to the meal plan."

"Boring! Don't let him badger you. He runs a tight ship and likes to keep his staff under his thumb, but he's got no soul or passion for this type of thing. He wouldn't recognize creativity if it bit him in the butt."

Tara sighed, knowing that trust had to be earned, and she'd gotten carried away today. It was just that for the past few years, other sous chefs had taken a back seat and allowed her to run the show. Philippe was not going to do that, and if she wanted to keep her job she'd have to toe the line. Even if it killed her. "I don't feel like going home. Want to grab a drink before we head home?"

"Sure. How about the Cock & Bull?"

She bit her lip and frowned. Was that the only bar in town? She'd been hoping to avoid dark and delicious Devon.

"Is that a problem?" Cindy asked. "I don't care where we go."

"No, it's not a problem. Matter-of-fact, I just arrived last night and don't know a thing about this place." She placed a smile on her face, not eager to let on to Cindy that she had met the bar manager, or whatever he was. Besides, it might be interesting to see if he still had any effect on her. Maybe it had been nerves, or a short lasting fever.

Cindy grinned. "Good, because it's the best bar in town. At least they have the two best looking bartenders in town. Kyle and Devon. Yummy."

"How interesting," Tara said, giving a careless shrug. "I have my car. You need a ride?"

"No, why don't you follow me?" Cindy got into her Honda CRV, and Tara followed closely in the Mini.

They found a parking lot on the next street and had to walk a half block, which nearly froze Tara's nose off. She knew her nose was probably red and runny, but it couldn't be helped. She wasn't used to this extreme weather.

When the two girls entered the bar, Tara saw Devon tossing bottles in the air and pouring drinks. Without a single drop of alcohol, she felt a light buzz. And the chill left her.

He looked up and nearly dropped the bottle he was holding, catching it in the nick of time. "Hey," he called out. "You found the place."

"It wasn't hidden." Tara smiled, and took a seat at the bar, and winked when Cindy nudged her.

"You've already met him?" she whispered. "Good work."

Tara kept her voice low when she answered. "My car skidded into a ditch, and he gave me a ride up the mountain."

"Lucky you. He could give me a ride all night long." Cindy put a hand over her mouth. "Oops. I shouldn't have said that. Besides, he can't keep his eyes off you."

"What are you girls having?" Devon asked, placing his palms on the counter as he leaned forward. "First one's on the house."

"You don't have to do that," Tara said quickly. "I already owe you."

Cindy nudged her foot. "You go girl," she whispered under her breath.

Devon grinned. "No, you don't. I don't get to come to a lady's rescue very often." He looked from one to the other. "So what will it be? I make a mean Cosmo."

"Uh, just a glass of chardonnay for me," Tara answered.

"I'll try that mean Cosmo," Cindy said, with a big smile for him.

He turned his back, which gave the women a nice view of his delectable rear. Tara felt her pulse soar. She grasped her hands in her lap because they itched to squeeze his very fine ass. She wasn't feverish exactly, but she was getting those erotic thoughts again. Maybe it would help if she didn't look at him.

She shifted her bar stool to face her new friend. "So, tell me about yourself. Have you worked here long?"

"Just over a year. I moved from Colorado." She looked at Devon and said loud enough for him to hear, "I love the mountain life. Beats smog and traffic, and all that stress. Don't you agree, Devon?"

"Nothing could be better," he answered, then turned to Tara. "So did you settle in all right?"

"Uh-huh." She glanced up, then dropped her eyes to study the counter. "I have the loveliest A-frame cottage. It's adorable." She took the glass of chardonnay out of his hands and their fingers touched.

Electric sparks flew between them. She flinched as though hit with a live current, and spilled a few drops of the wine. "Oh, I'm sorry," she said, turning a few shades of pink. "Did you just feel that? I got a shock."

"Yeah. Must be the dry air." He slid the Cosmo to Cindy and picked up a bar towel to wipe away the wine.

She licked her lips and watched his hands move over the counter, wondering how they'd feel moving over her body. Oh, my gosh! Those crazy thoughts again. Whatever this guy did to her, it had to stop.

Cindy took a big sip from her Cosmo, unaware of Tara's distress. Her attention diverted when another young man arrived.

"Hey, Kyle. It's time you turned up," Devon said, glancing at his watch. "Happy hour was busy tonight. But I managed alone."

"Told you business would pick up." Kyle slid under the counter, and quickly got to work.

Cindy whispered, "That's the other one. Kyle—his brother. Isn't he gorgeous? But he's dating one of the ski instructors."

"Don't you have a boyfriend?" Tara asked. "A pretty girl like you. I'd think you'd have your pick."

"I dated someone for a while, but we broke up a few months ago. Now—nobody." She grinned. "But I'm looking. Definitely looking. Need someone to keep me warm on these cold chilly nights."

"Not me," Tara told her. "I had a boyfriend in Beverly Hills, where I worked before. We dated for six months then I found out that he was still married. He'd told me he was divorced, but no, just separated. Then he went on vacation and took his wife. I found out about it a couple of weeks later."

"Ouch. That was a bad experience," Cindy said, making a sympathetic face.

"You think?" Tara sighed. "Well, I was ready to move on anyway, and then this job came up. Perfect timing."

"I'm glad. You're going to be fun to work with."

"You say that now, but I'm pretty demanding. I expect a lot, but give a lot too."

"That's fine by me." Cindy tapped her empty glass. "Kyle, could I have another one please?" She batted her eyelashes. "It's a Cosmo."

As Kyle made Cindy's drink, Devon turned his attention on Tara. His chocolate eyes skimmed over her face, and trailed lower. "Another chardonnay?"

Her skin flushed, but she nodded, trying to appear calm, cool, like a normal woman having a normal conversation with a nice looking bartender. Not like some hot-to-trot floozie that had an itch needing to be scratched. "Sure." She pushed the empty glass at him. "I have nothing to rush back home too."

The girls stayed and had a light dinner, played some pool, and chased off a few men, and all the while, Tara could feel Devon's eyes on her, causing her blood to run hot.

She was not a promiscuous person, but every time their eyes met she felt a low tug in her belly, and a tingling sensation that made her want to squirm. She knew it meant only one thing—she wanted him. Plain and simple. There was enough heat between them to start another California wildfire. Too bad he only dated city girls.

CHAPTER FIVE

Devon was good and pissed. He hadn't liked it at all when Tara and her friend got up from the bar and decided to shoot pool. The place was hopping with horny men and they were wriggling their butts over the table, while guys ogled them. As if they didn't know. They'd laughed, teasing the men, and Tara had flashed those gorgeous green eyes of hers and kept tossing her mane of hair around. She'd also shown way too much cleavage as she angled her hot body to make the right shot.

Gawd almighty, but he'd ogled too. More than that, he'd gotten so pumped up he had to stay behind the counter so nobody would see he was sporting a big one. Fucking hell! He owned the bar; he couldn't go around with a hard-on for one of his customers.

Times were bad enough. They bought the business from the existing owners, but the rent they paid for their main street address was astronomical, and this summer had been a dud. Kyle didn't seem to care--he left the worrying to Devon. Well, perhaps that's what big brothers were for.

If Kyle ran things, they'd lose money so fast, they'd have to shut down. He liked to give away free drinks to all the pretty young girls on the weekends, and Devon was forced to put a stop to that. They now had "happy hour" half-priced drinks and appetizers from four until seven, which seemed to make everyone happy, especially Devon when he counted the cash at the end of the night.

He watched Tara saunter over to the bar. She was wearing a crisp white blouse with the first three buttons undone, grey dress slacks that fit her ass a little too darn good, and a baby blue, cashmere sweater. Her curly, auburn hair fell below her shoulders, and she had a confident walk. It was almost a strut like the great looking models do in TV ads.

He swallowed hard and tried not to stare. The first time he'd seen her she'd been wearing a heavy wool jacket so he hadn't known what she had going on underneath. Now, his eyes had x-ray vision, and he knew the shape of her breasts, the tightness of her nipples, and could only imagine how they'd feel in his hands.

Shit. There went his dick again. Just when he'd had it almost under control.

"Hi." She smiled. "Can I have another glass of wine?"

"Haven't you had enough already?" Devon snapped. "You've had two."

Kyle looked up from washing a glass. "Give the lady a drink. Since when do we keep count around here?" He smiled at Tara. "I'm Kyle. Are you the girl Devon gave a ride to?"

"I am." She held out her hand. "Tara Reynolds. I'm the new pastry chef at the Grande."

"Mmm," Kyle winked. "You look kind of sweet yourself."

"Kyle, shut up." Devon gave him a shove. "That's no way to talk to a customer."

"I don't mind," Tara said with a grin. "At least he's nicer than you are."

"I'm nice enough," Devon replied. "You want a drink? By all means. Don't let me stop you if you want to get drunk."

Her emerald eyes popped wide open. "Is this how you treat your clientele? If so, I'm surprised you have any at all." She put her hand on her hips, which only further outlined her small waist and generous breasts. "Is this a drinking establishment or did I stumble into the wrong place?"

"Uh," he felt a flash of heat from his cock upward. "I'm just trying to keep things orderly here."

She leaned her elbows on the bar which gave him a nice look down her cleavage. "Do I look disorderly to you?"

He gulped. "No, not yet. Just don't want you stirring up the natives. They're all over you." At her amused look, he turned away. "Let me get your chardonnay. As long as you're sure you can drive home."

She smiled. "If I can't, I'll find someone who can."

He thrust the glass in her hand. "Enjoy. I'm sure you'll find plenty of horn-dogs who'd be happy to oblige."

"Horn-dogs?" she laughed. "And that bothers you why?" She leaned her back against the bar and surveyed the crowd. "Last I heard, you only date city girls."

"Seems like a good idea. That way they aren't hanging around all the time while I'm working."

"Good. Then it shouldn't bother you one way or another if I'm here, or not here. Or if I drink myself silly and some poor stiff has to drive me home. Makes no difference to you. Right?"

"Right. Doesn't affect me either way. You want to flirt—go right ahead. Guys can't take their eyes off you. Have fun. Knock yourself out."

"What guys?" she asked, flipping her hair.

"The ones that are shooting pool with your friend there."

"Oh, yeah. They seem nice. One of them offered to give me ski instructions if I baked him a pie."

Devon's jaw tensed, and he gritted his teeth. "You offered to bake him a pie?" He looked down his nose at her. "Which guy?"

"The cute one with the long, shaggy, blonde hair."

"That guy can't ski worth shit. You want to learn, you should ski with me."

"That's odd. He said he was a ski instructor. You're a bartender. I think Josh might be a better choice." She sipped on her wine. "He offered to teach me this weekend. Of course, I have skied some, but I mostly stick to the beginner slopes."

"I'm in the ski patrol." Devon said thickly. He was so choked he could hardly speak. What the hell was wrong with him, anyway? Why should he care who taught her to ski or ate her damn pie?

"Yeah? That's nice, but it doesn't mean you know how to teach. Right?"

"I didn't say I could teach, but I could ski circles around these jerks."

"That right? What would they say about that?"

"They might say I made the Olympics, then again, they might say I shattered my leg in three places." He left to attend to a few people, but he could feel her eyes on him.

Why the hell had he told her that? He didn't want her damn sympathy, that's for sure. It was ancient history. Didn't matter anymore. The back of his neck felt hot, and everything about this woman rubbed him the wrong way. She got him going, that's for damn sure. Made him want to grab fistfuls of her hair and pull that sexy mouth of hers down. The image made him hard again. He started counting change in the cash register to keep his mind from thinking about the stuff he'd like to do to her.

Her girlfriend came over and Devon heard her say she was going home.

"I'll be leaving right behind you," Tara said. "See you in the morning."

As soon as the friend left, Tara took a seat at the bar. "Excuse me," she called. "Sorry to bother you when you are so obviously busy."

Devon turned and strode over. "You want another drink?"

"No, I think I've had enough. What time does this place close?"

"When the crowd thins. Probably about an hour from now."

She looked at him. Cocked her head, and gave him a half smile. "You want me to wait?"

"Wait for what?" he asked stupidly.

"For you to drive me home." She glanced around the bar, her eyes on Josh who stood leaning against a wall as if waiting for her to return.

She turned back to him, and the way her eyes looked him up and down, sent shocks waves through his system. "I told you that you drank too much."

"I'm not drunk," she answered in a soft, sexy voice.

"Then why don't you drive your own car?" Damn, he wanted to grab her and plant a big one right on those tasty looking lips.

"It won't be as much fun." She smiled slowly. "Besides, I heard you like city woman, and that's where I'm from. Fresh from Rodeo Drive."

"You're pushy, you know that." He started to mop the counter, just so he didn't have to look at her. Last thing he needed was a hot chick looking for a good time hanging around his place. Especially if she'd set her cap on him.

"No, I'm not. I never stick around long enough to become a nuisance. Probably a year from now, I'll be at another Grande location. It's good for my career to keep moving."

His gaze left the counter, slid up over her beautiful breasts and landed on her face. He quirked a brow. "I don't do a year. A week at most. Usually a lot shorter."

She laughed. "Neither do I. You're safe from me."

"So, you still want me to take you home?" He looked at her full mouth again, and his mind wandered to lusty places.

"Only if you want to. I could call it a night. It's getting late and I need to be on my toes tomorrow. Still trying to make a good impression, you know what I mean?"

"You leave an impression, all right." He wiped his hands. "I'll tell Kyle that he needs to close." He glanced around the bar. "Give me a half hour then I'll meet you around back."

"All right." She sauntered over to Josh and whispered something to him. He shrugged, walked over to a group of girls, and asked one to dance. The young woman jumped up at once, and Josh whirled her around the floor. Some honky-tonk sound was playing on the juke box.

Twenty minutes later, Devon snuck up behind Tara. He put his hands on her hips and whispered in her ear. "I can leave now. You ready to go?"

She turned around and her face was inches from his. She looked into his eyes. "I'm ready. Willing and able."

CHAPTER SIX

The minute they stepped outside, Devon pulled her into his arms. She lifted her face and put her hands around his neck. "What am I doing?" she whispered then pulled his mouth toward hers. "I'm usually very cautious who I get involved with," she said between kisses, "but you drive me wild."

He crushed her mouth and opened her lips with one thrust of his tongue. He plunged inside and she didn't mind. She didn't want gentle kisses, she needed soul deep, gut wrenching, fathomless kisses that seared every nerve, inside and out. She had no idea why her lips were glued to someone she barely knew. He was attractive, but this was not attraction. It was a must have. Had been from the moment they met.

It should have scared her silly, but she was hapless to stop the demanding urge sweeping over her every time his tongue touched hers, when his fingertips brushed her nipple, or when his hips rubbed against her. Nor did she want to stop it. This rush of adrenalin, or whatever the heck it was, had to be the most thrilling thing she'd ever experienced.

She wanted it to continue, at least for a few more hours. She'd deal with the aftermath tomorrow. It certainly wouldn't be heartache this time around. She didn't know Devon well enough or long enough for any true feelings to develop. This was lust. Pure and simple.

She grabbed his hand, holding it against her breast. It felt warm, and even in the icy air, she didn't need to zip up her jacket. Devon's kisses had heated her though and through. "Guess we should stop this or we won't make it home. Do you want to drive or shall I?"

"Take your car and I'll follow." His eyes were like melted honey as they lingered on her mouth. He pulled her to him once again and gave her another long kiss, as if he couldn't get enough. He murmured, "It'll be more practical in the morning."

"Sure." She pulled back, heart hammering like a roadrunner, and offered him a bright smile. "It's only a couple of blocks. I'm good." She slid into her car, and he jumped into his truck and was right on her heels.

She parked in the carport, grabbed her handbag, and stepped out. Devon was there to take her hand. They entered the dark cabin from the side door and were in a mud room. She flipped on a light, kicked off her boots, and dropped her bag, then turned around to reach for him.

Devon fumbled for her coat, his fingers working quickly. Then his hands covered her breasts, causing her to sigh deeply. "Oh, my. This is insane. Crazy." She licked her lips and didn't move his hands. "But I don't want to stop. Do you?"

"Not a chance," he said before grinding his mouth to hers in a hungry, demanding kiss. He was tugging at her clothes, trying to get her shirt undone, and acting with want comparable to her own. They didn't even know each other, but it was so physical between them—enough sparks and electricity to light up the Fourth of July.

Giving in to the insanity, she put her hand around his neck and backed into the kitchen, never breaking the kiss. He had the first five buttons undone, now pulling the shirt out of her slacks. Hurry, hurry, she breathed. Want, need, budded inside of her. Devon O'Reilley was the most dangerous man she'd ever known—a man that had her thinking with her body instead of her head.

She would have to be very careful if they did get involved. Offering him her body, but withholding her heart. It was tricky work, and had backfired on her before. Forcing those thoughts out of her mind, she moved her hips forward, making contact with the bulge in his straining jeans. She rubbed up against him, not caring what happened beyond tonight. Making love to him, that was all that mattered.

Her back was to the counter, with no place left to go. He pushed her shirt open, bent his head, and sucked on a nipple through the lacy, silk bra. She moaned her pleasure, and nipped at his shoulder, not wanting these delicious, exciting vibes to ever end. No man had ever thrilled her the way he did now. Every touch sent a pleasurable jolt, and her entire body hummed with need and expectation.

Devon put his hand between her thighs, forcing them apart. He held his hand at her heated junction, making her hotter. Wetter. Desire flowed through her, from the tips of her curled toes to the center of her being.

His other hand pushed her breast up and over the cup of her bra, and his tongue played with her nipple, tasting it, teasing it until she withered against him, pushing herself forward into the palm of his hand.

"You want this?" he whispered huskily.

Nothing had prepared her for this moment. It was beyond her comprehension that she'd be doing these things, but she murmured against his ear, "Yes. Very much. I don't know why, but I do." She stroked him and unzipped his fly. "And you?"

"God, yes."

She shuddered, and tried to shake off whatever demon had possessed her. Instead, only warmth swept over her flesh. Giving into the pleasure, she pleaded, "Now, quickly." Her hand slipped around his cock, wanting the heat of it inside her. Now. She gasped. "Before I change my mind. Take me."

Devon unzipped her pants and slid them down her legs, closely followed by her lace undies. She shivered and lifted her arms. Quickly, Devon picked her up and placed her bare bottom on the kitchen counter. She removed her sweater and blouse, then unhooked her bra, letting her clothes fall to the floor.

She took his head in her hands and kissed him gently, loving the taste of his lips, the warmth and sweetness of his mouth. He broke the kiss and licked her belly, then ran his tongue along the inside of her thighs. "Devon…"

"It's all good, Tara. Trust me."

His assurance swept aside her doubt and she fisted his hair in her hands. Following her instincts, she pulled him closer as he kissed her sensitive inner thighs, widening her legs in invitation. She jumped, startled as his warm mouth settled over her most private part. She cried out the minute his tongue touched her—the sensation brand new. Nothing in her past had prepared her for this. It was insanely erotic, intensely arousing, and explosive. She stared down at the top of his head, her hands in his hair, so dark between her pale legs. His tongue flicked over her sensitive nub, another flick, and with a small whimper of surprise, she came.

Then froze-- her entire body suspended in motion. A moment after her release came a deep, overwhelming shame.

"Oh, no. I'm so sorry. This has never happened to me before." She pushed his head away, and he slowly looked up.

"You're apologizing?" he asked with a slow, sexy tilt of his lips. "Why? Enjoying sex is good. I want you to sit back and relax." He ran his hands up her thighs. "We're just getting started. I'm good all night."

All night?

He pulled her forward and wrapped her in his arms. He kissed her cheeks tenderly. "What's the matter? You have tears in your eyes." He kissed her eyelids. "I didn't do anything wrong, did I?" When she didn't answer, he pulled back, a frown on his puzzled face. "Don't tell me that was your first time?"

"No, I'm not a virgin if that's what you mean," she said and released a shuddering breath. "But it's the first time like that. You know…with your mouth I mean." She felt her cheeks warm. "I'm sorry."

"You're a tongue virgin?" He chuckled, smoothing her hair back from her forehead. His chest practically puffed out with testosterone. "Wait, Tara, darlin'—there's lots more. Why don't we get a little more comfortable? You got a bed somewhere?"

"I don't think this is a good idea, Devon. I'm not feeling so well." She pushed at his shoulders, needing to distance herself. Her body wanted more all right, but she felt feverish, and flushed with shame. "Maybe I did have too much too drink."

He stepped back and she could see the disappointment in his eyes. "No, you didn't. You're not drunk, and you knew exactly what you wanted."

She looked down at his mouth, his lips--too self-conscious to maintain eye contact for long. "Yes, I did want you. I wanted this. As much as you did." She touched his face. "I've never felt anything like it." She licked her lips, her lower body humming back to life at the idea of more. "I couldn't control myself."

"You just had a tiny appetizer, Tara. That's all." He smiled. "I think you can handle the full course."

She looked down and saw that Devon was almost bursting out of his shorts. His jeans were at his ankles, and his erection begged for attention. She closed her eyes, afraid to look, afraid to want more. She needed to regain control. The way she desired him was totally scary. It was wild, primitive, and distorted. Hell, she barely knew the guy and she'd wanted him everywhere.

After a couple of seconds, she heard him step away and heard his fly zip up.

"I'll leave," he said tightly.

Her eyes widened. "I'm sorry. Really, Devon. This wasn't very nice of me. I invited you to a party, and I came and you didn't."

"Well, darling, as you say, I don't date the local girls. So no harm done. We'll just chalk this up to experience and stay well clear of each other." He turned and walked away. "Don't get up. I'll see myself out."

The minute she heard the sound of his Jeep tearing out of the driveway, she jumped down from the counter, picked up her discarded clothes, and scurried upstairs to her bedroom. She shut the door and ran to the bathroom to look in the full-length mirror.

What happened to her tonight? Her cheeks were flushed, her eyes unnaturally bright. She looked like she was on something, but she didn't do drugs and never would. Her heart pounded in her chest, and she rubbed at it absently. She fingered a little spot on her chest and saw that it was pink. Like a mosquito bite, except it wasn't itchy, just annoying.

She took a shower, but nothing could make her forget his kisses and the flick of his tongue. The fact that she'd climaxed when his tongue was inside her, made her want to die right there. She turned the shower to cold, splashing it on her face, between her legs, wanting to wash away the memory and the heat that came as she remembered all of it.

How could she ever face him again? She'd have to avoid his bar from here on in. And if she ever saw him on the street, well, she wouldn't look his way. He was probably kicking himself right now, cursing the day he'd ever offered her a ride.

* * *

Devon was cursing all right. His cock was still fighting for release, and his jeans were chaffing it badly. The last time he'd gotten so close and been so quickly shut down, well he couldn't remember the last time. Maybe he'd been all of fourteen or something.

What was that girls' name? Maggie? Cute little Maggie Sullivan with strawberry blonde pigtails and freckles on her nose. She'd been the first girl in his class to grow boobs, and by the time he got a date with her several years later, her pigtails were gone and so was her virginity. When he tried to get to first base, she'd punched him in the nose and told him that she'd thought he might be different.

He'd felt bad for her but worse for himself. He was just as horny as the other boys and had only wanted what everyone else was getting.

He felt a little like that now. When he looked up from the inside of Tara's pretty thighs and saw tears in her eyes, he'd felt guilty--like he'd been stealing candy from a baby. Obviously she'd had one too many and he'd taken advantage of the fact—no, that was not true. She had wanted him, had invited him home.

Obviously, she wasn't as sexually experienced as him and hadn't been prepared. She probably only knew men who were one dimensional lovers.

So, she'd been revved up and enjoyed his tongue a little too much. Well, he'd have enjoyed teaching her a lot more about how a man could please a woman, but if she wanted that kind of education, she'd have to come asking, because he wasn't going to give her another opportunity to shoot his dick down.

It was still standing at full alert and when he tried to shift his weight to loosen his crotch, the pain in his butt-cheek flared again.

If it was sciatica, he'd be in for a long, dreary winter. He glanced at the cloudless sky and saw the sliver of a moon and a million brilliant stars shining bright. It was a beautiful night, and it would have been even more damn beautiful in that bed of hers, wrapped between her warm thighs. Now, he had to go home to his brother and best friend, Mogul, the hairy beast that slept with him most nights, gave him unconditional love, and never asked for anything besides a good scratch and a cheap meal.

The place was dark when he got home. Kyle must have stayed the night at Lisa's. At least one of them was getting lucky. He switched on the light, and Mogul slumbered over to him, rubbing against his legs.

"Hey, there, boy. You want somethin' to eat?"

He cracked the door open. "Go take a leak, and I'll get your treat."

The old mongrel, half Collie, half bear, went out on the deck and left a patch of yellow snow in the corner. He ran back inside and sat on his haunches, waiting for his reward. Devon tossed him a couple of dog cookies and popped open a bottle of beer.

He got a fire going and sat in an old, comfy chair with his feet on an ottoman. The dog sat next to him, happily eating his snacks, enjoying his home, the warmth of the fire, Devon's company.

Why couldn't a woman be more like a dog?

CUPID

Oh, my, oh my—that had been embarrassing. When that big fellow lifted her up on the kitchen counter without any clothes on, I put my hands over my eyes and dashed into a kitchen cupboard. Lucky for me it was the pantry, so I had some really good snacks while they were doing the deed.

Even at my age, I still get uncomfortable with this stuff. Being a gentleman, I always divert my eyes, but my ears are not so easy to turn off. I hear the grunting and the groaning and other noises, but since I was in the cupboard I nibbled on crunchy potato chips and a handful of cashews too.

There were slats in the cupboard and when I sneaked a peek, I saw the back of his head between the lady's thighs. I wonder what he was looking for. Well, whatever it was, she screamed out his name, and then got all worked up about something. He left shortly after, so I guess that first love-making session, if that's what it had been, had not worked out as well as I had hoped.

Oh, dear! This is so disturbing. I'm going to have to take a long nap and try to sort this out. Why can't everyone just fall in love and be done with it? Why do they have to fight it, kicking and screaming, every inch of the way?

Heck, if it were me, and I met a lovely little Cupid darling, I would welcome her with open arms and be the most loving, unselfish Cupid she'd ever met and make sure she'd never leave. I would share my special hoard of sweets, and buy her red roses, and feed her raw oysters and love her for eternity.

But that's just me. Humans are a different species entirely. They like to argue and fight. They have big egos and tiny dicks, and always seem mad about something. How many times have I seen the poor girls cry? I comfort them the best that I can, and pat them on the backs of their heads and say soothing words like 'don't cry dear, Cupid will make everything all right'.

But it's like they never hear me. Like I'm invisible or something. I can see myself just fine. Why can't other people?

CHAPTER SEVEN

Tara had a hard time getting to sleep but when she did she slept soundly, and woke up in the morning feeling relaxed, her muscles fluid, tension gone. She stretched and yawned, smiling happily as she glanced out the bedroom window to see the snow-capped mountain.

She'd had quite a day yesterday, yes, quite a day. She'd made some big decisions which had won the respect of her immediate team but caused a tiff with her direct boss. Well, he had to recognize the fact that she was an executive chef too, and the dessert buffet and pastries were her responsibility, not his. Sure, he was her superior, and she needed to toe the line, but only so far—after all they'd hired her for her creativity.

She also made a new friend, Cindy, who had a thing for Kyle. Devon's brother.

Holy Crap!!! Devon. Oh no, oh no, oh no! She squeezed her eyes tight. Please say it wasn't so. She hadn't done that, had she? It was a dream. That's all. Just a figment of her creative imagination. She didn't have casual sex with guys she barely knew, and she most certainly did not do what she dreamed about. *My gosh, no!* She'd experienced that kind of foreplay before, but she'd never gotten off on it, really. No, she was more the straight sex kind of girl, male on top of female or vice versa.

No way in hell had she climaxed on that man's tongue. Didn't happen. Couldn't happen. It was one of those dreams that seem so real you almost believed it. Like walking naked in a crowd. Nobody does that, but it's a common enough dream.

She laughed and got out of bed. Thank heavens she didn't engage in that kind of sexual activity. Imagine waking up knowing that you'd creamed somebody's face. No thank you. Especially when you weren't in a committed relationship. Different if you were married or had known that person for a long, long time. Then anything was acceptable, and variety was the spice of life. Good for the bedroom, healthy in keeping a marriage alive. But with a guy she'd only just met. Hell no!

She picked up her undergarments and shirt and tossed them in a clothes bin, then hung up her slacks. Strange that she hadn't done that last night when she went to bed.

Had she undressed here or had that part of the dream been real? The part where she'd been exchanging passionate kisses with Devon, and he'd followed her home and come into her kitchen?

If so, had they had a glass of wine? She'd check and see if there were two glasses in the kitchen sink. Two glasses could mean one thing, that yes, he had been in her house, but it didn't mean she'd opened her thighs to him.

One thing, not two. She ran into the kitchen and didn't see any evidence of wine, glasses, or anything out of place. She was safe.

She made her coffee and went in to shower, allowing the warm water to roll over her very relaxed body and wash away any negative thoughts. This was her second day on the job and the beginning of an exciting adventure. She figured she might be good for a year, possibly longer, if she enjoyed it as much as she expected. She'd needed a change, and getting out of the city had been a brilliant idea.

She turned off the shower and stepped out of the stall, catching a glimpse of herself in the mirror. She remembered Devon's hands on her breasts, the warmth of his breath as he sucked her nipple through the lacy bra. She remembered him lifting her, setting her on the kitchen counter.

Then what? She closed her eyes as quick visual flashes flooded her brain. He'd spread her legs, and his tongue, that long, devilish tongue flickered in--once, twice, he'd hit and scored, sending her over the moon and back.

Oh. My. God. It hadn't been a dream after all. It was a nightmare.

What could she do to undo what she'd done? Even the thought didn't make sense any more than the reality of what she'd allowed this near stranger to do. It was unthinkable but undeniable. She'd done it. Had it been straight sex, she could handle that—no problemo, but it was the other thing.

Maybe it wasn't too late to put in for a transfer. She could tell the top management team at Cascade Resorts that she'd made a colossal error, and she hated the mountains, and the high atmosphere did strange things to her head. She had to be relocated immediately—

preferably someplace far away. Did they have any openings in Dubai?

She groaned, and rubbed her head. Couldn't even blame a hangover. Well, she would push it into the back closet of her mind, turn the key, and refuse to think about it. That's what she'd do. It had worked for her before, and she was quite the expert at ignoring things that made her feel bad.

Still, the joy had seeped out of the morning, and even her coffee didn't taste the same. She made herself an egg on toast, ate it without tasting a thing, then put the dishes away. She dressed in a black knit skirt with black leggings and an ivory colored turtleneck with a wide, black belt. She pulled her long, sometimes unruly hair into a French braid, and applied her make-up with a light touch. She found her coat and pulled on her knee high boots.

Today, if she really tried hard, she might be able to make the Sous Chef angry enough to fire her. All she had to do was not follow his direction and do whatever the heck she pleased. Tara could manage that easily enough.

She showed up fifteen minutes late and totally ignored the list of desserts scheduled for the conference attendees today. If they thought they'd been treated well yesterday, well just wait until they got a load of what she had planned for them today.

From the time she arrived until the time she left, she worked along with her caterers and didn't take time out for lunch. They had sticky buns, pumpkin muffins, moist, thick slices of banana/apple/raison bread, and trays of fresh fruit for their morning meeting. Not done yet, she added a selection of mini quiches and freshly baked croissants, some plain, others with dark chocolate.

For lunch she served a strawberry-blueberry trifle, fancy éclairs, and a warm apple torte with cinnamon ice cream. The afternoon snack consisted of a selection of cookies, brownies, and a tart with mocha crust, white chocolate mousse, and orange cream. Later, a chocolate lava cake with cherry sauce, mini tiramisus, and almond amaretto cheesecakes capped off the evening dinner.

By the time she finished, the Sous Chef was hopping mad, the waiters grumbling, and the catering staff dropping like flies. She figured she'd cooked her goose for sure, and she'd be able to slink out of town without ever having to face Devon again.

Unfortunately, it was not to be. Just when Phillip was ripping her a new one, Marc Florian appeared to say that the CEO of ISE, the International Solar Energy company, had been so impressed by the food and the staff that they'd already booked for the following year.

Phillip shot her an angry look, then turned on his heels and flounced off.

"Everything okay here?" Marc asked. "What did Phillip have to say?"

"Not much. He was concerned that I'd been working the staff too hard, and that maybe I'd overstepped the boundaries just a teeny bit."

"I noticed how hard you've all been working the past couple of days." He said it with a smile, which could only mean he was pleased. She'd stepped on everyone's toes, created havoc in the kitchen and out, and he was pleased? Shoot me now, she thought.

He continued, "Phillip informed me that you'd gone over budget, but I'm happy to say that your initiative paid off." He looked proud as a peacock as he stroked his mustache. "You're going to be an asset around here, Tara. Good job. Keep it up."

"You mean, you don't want to fire me?" She frowned. "I didn't do anything I was told to do. I probably blew the budget big time."

"You used your creativity to impress the people that matter and bring in repeat business. I'm very pleased with you."

There was that word again—pleased. She hadn't meant for that to happen, how could she make it stop? What did she have to do? Poison someone?

"Thank you." She took two steps back. "I guess I'll see you in the morning then."

"Yes, you can come in an hour later. You deserve it after working so hard."

Sheesh, the guy didn't know how to run a staff, he only saw dollar signs dangling before his eyes. He should fire her on the spot. She'd have done it.

"Thanks, Marc. I appreciate it." She sighed heavily, wondering if this was her fate after all. She did like it here and loved her sweet cabin, and now it certainly looked like she would have to hang around for a while. It might be impossible to avoid Devon forever, but she wouldn't go out of her way to see him either.

She was putting on her coat when Cindy came up behind her. "Wow, that was quite a day we had. Mr. Florian told us all how well we'd done and to keep up the good work." She grinned. "Guess we should celebrate. Want to go for a drink?"

"As long as it's not the Cock & Bull. I'd rather try someplace new."

"Really? Looked like you were having a good time last night. How long did you stay after I left?"

"Maybe half an hour."

"So, which one was it? The cute ski instructor or Devon, the bartender?"

"It wasn't anyone. I drove myself home and slept alone." Well, that much was true. Cindy didn't need to know about the little indiscretion in between.

"Boring," she said with a smile. "There's a nice bar at the hotel down the street that has music and dancing. Are you up for it?"

"Dancing? Not tonight. I've been on my feet all day."

"Me too," Cindy replied. "But I've still got energy to burn."

"Sorry. Count me out." Tara stifled a yawn. "I could use a nice quiet drink somewhere then I'm off to bed."

"I know just the place. It's a piano bar at the Fairmont Hotel with a good clientele. Since it's not a local hangout, the pickin's are better there. We don't want to fall in love with a ski bum, do we?"

"Not if I can help it," Tara answered, feeling that pang again in her chest. "I'm done with losers. The next guy I'm going to get hung up on, well, he better have a good job, love children, be kind, generous and faithful, and enjoy Tapioca sex."

CHAPTER EIGHT

"Tapioca? What does that mean? It sounds awfully boring." Cindy asked as they walked to the parking lot.

"Just nothing kinky."

"Oh. Well, I agree with that." She glanced at Tara. "I think. Depends on what's kinky."

"Well, I like things normal with very little deviation. Call me old-fashioned, but I still like the old missionary position best or me on top."

"Come on, girl." Cindy rolled her eyes. "You should experiment more."

"No, thanks. I've slept with four guys and they were all good. I have no complaints on that account." Tara lowered her voice, "But I don't get off every time. Actually, not often at all."

"A lot of women don't. Me, almost always."

"Why? How? I mean, how come some women do and others don't?"

"You're asking me this? How do I know? It just happens."

"Hmm." Tara stopped next to her car. "I'm just not that sexual, I guess. I want a guy who'll be more like my best friend. Someone I can talk to and curl up with at night."

"That's nice too, but I want fireworks every time."

"Too much trouble," she answered. "I don't want explosions, just feel-good sex. Nice and easy." Tara opened her car door. "I'm only having one drink tonight, then I'm off. Lead the way."

The piano bar was rocking by the time they arrived. Every table was taken, but after several minutes they managed to get their drinks and stand next to the bar.

"You call this a quiet drink?" Tara shouted over the singing.

"Uh—maybe I forgot the quiet part." Cindy grinned. "But it is fun!"

Someone standing next to Cindy, obviously on the make, struck up a conversation. Cindy responded, perfectly happy to be chatted up.

Tara sipped her drink and glanced around the room. A few guys tried to catch her eye, but she wasn't in the mood. The clientele did look more promising than at the Cock & Bull, if a professional man was on your short list. Not that she was interested--it was the very last thing on her mind. She intended to take a nice long break from love and heart break and all that stuff. She should blame her last boyfriend, Jeff, she supposed. After all, he'd lied and cheated, and even if he hadn't broken her heart, he'd bruised it bad.

"Tara!" Someone at another table waved at her. "How're you doing?"

It was Ken, the realtor. She waved back. "Good." She smiled and raised her glass to him in a salute. A minute later, he was at her side.

"So, you're settling in okay? How's the house? Any problems?"

"No, none at all. Everything's good. Thanks for asking."

"Can I buy you ladies a drink?" he asked, eying her friend.

Cindy gave him a big smile. "Hi. I'm Cindy."

"Ken Johnson." He grinned and stuck out his hand. "Do you work with Tara?"

"I do. I'm an apprentice, not nearly as experienced as our sous chef here. Except in some things," she said with a laugh. "So how do you two know each other?"

"She rented one of my properties. I'm with Admiral Realty." He pulled a business card from his wallet. "Keep this in case you're ever looking."

"For what?" she said and gave him a flirty look.

His neck and cheeks flooded with color. "For anything. What are you drinking?"

Tara watched them and could see the sparks flying. Could it really be that easy? One minute you're standing alone in a crowd of people wondering if you'll ever meet that special someone, and then you look up and there he is.

She put a hand on Cindy's arm and whispered in her ear. "I'm going home. I'm exhausted. You stay and have fun--he's a nice guy."

"See ya," she said, her eyes twinkling. "Not Tapioca, I hope?" she whispered, darting a look at Ken.

Tara shrugged. "Goodnight, Ken. I've had a long day. Will you take care of Cindy if I leave?"

"With pleasure." He winked at Cindy. "Nice seeing you again, Tara."

With a sense of relief, Tara left the bar, intending to drive straight home. Unfortunately, she had to go by the Cock & Bull since it was on the same road she had to travel. A car space opened in front of her, and she didn't know how, but her car just seemed to slip into the vacant spot.

Her heart hammered painfully, and she felt flushed with heat. What the hell was she doing? Why were her feet leading her into the place she had no wish to go?

She kept her head low, as she stumbled toward the bar and slid onto a bar stool. She didn't look up but she sensed Devon standing in front of her. "You want something?" he asked in a voice as smooth as Velveeta cheese.

"Yes, but I'm not sure what."

He turned around and came back with a shot glass in his hand.

She took the offered drink. "What is it?"

"A Slippery Nipple."

Her mouth opened then shut quickly. She looked into his face and saw his lips twitching, his eyes sparkling with mirth. She clasped a hand over her mouth then laughter bubbled up inside of her and came out in hysterical spurts. When she could catch her breath, she knocked the drink back and wiped her mouth.

"Not bad. Can I have a second?"

"You know what happens when you drink too much," he replied and poured her another.

"It wasn't the drink. I don't know what it was, but you're right. I knew what I was doing. Right up until, you know…"

"Uh-huh." He looked away. "I didn't expect to see you back here so soon."

"I didn't intend to come…I mean come in here tonight." She giggled, extremely embarrassed. "But I was driving past and my car just seemed to stop. Weird, isn't it?"

"Interesting car you've got there. It gets you into a lot of trouble, doesn't it?"

She locked eyes with him. "I should sell it, but it does liven things up." She licked her lips. "Anyway, now that I'm here, I should apologize for last night. That was very bad behavior on my part and it won't happen again."

"Which part?" His lips curled with amusement. "The before, the during, or the after?"

Tara felt her cheeks warm, but she didn't look away. "All of it. I mean, I don't know you very well. You seem like a great guy, but I shouldn't have invited you to my home. That's not the kind of girl I am. Or want to be."

"So you said last night." He put an elbow on the counter and rested his head in his hand, studying her face. "I think you're lying to yourself. Inside, there is a great, fun-loving girl just dying to get out."

"Better not be. I have plans for my future and they don't include having fun."

He cocked a brow. "That's ridiculous. Why do you insist on being so uptight? What's wrong with working hard and playing hard too?"

"I don't know. It's just not the way I do things."

"How do you do things?" He eyed her. "Obviously not like last night."

"No." She lowered her voice, wanting him to understand that she wasn't a tease. She was simply different from most girls he met working the bar. "My mom died when I was sixteen, and she didn't get to live all her dreams, so I decided nothing was going to stop me from mine. I wanted a job that included travel and I've got that. I wanted to do something that I enjoyed, was good at, and made the world a happier place, so I became a pastry chef. My delicious delicacies bring pleasure to people and that makes me gooey inside."

"What else makes you gooey?" he asked quietly.

"Babies. They're so tiny and delicious, and I want to eat them up." She laughed. "Just kidding. But one day I'm going to marry and have several."

"So what are you waiting for?"

"I keep falling for the wrong kind of guy. And when I get too close to someone, I feel suffocated and have to get away." She gazed into his eyes. "Isn't that weird?"

"Sounds to me like you don't know what you want. When you do, I'm sure it'll all work out."

She slurped down her drink and pushed the glass away. "Thanks for the drink and letting me apologize. I wanted to clear the air since we're living in this small village together."

"We're not living together, but I get what you mean." He tipped his head at her. "Until next time."

She took her money out of her wallet. "What next time?"

"The next time you want to give it a try. Just tell me when."

"You've got a really big ego, you know that!" She tossed down a twenty. "Keep the change, and you can call us even."

The sound of his laughter followed her out the door.

CHAPTER NINE

He watched her leave and then turned to the few stragglers still sitting at the bar. "Drink up, everybody. It's time to close up. We can all reconvene back here tomorrow."

He heard their grumbling, but they finished their drinks, paid their bills, and headed out into the cold. The locals who frequented his bar knew there was no official closing time. If the place was busy, they could stay and drink all night. On quiet nights, he closed early. They respected the unspoken rules and gave no argument.

He locked the doors behind them, cleaned up, counted the cash, and turned out the lights. Kyle had left early, but Devon was glad he'd been the one to stay late. Especially since Tara had come in to apologize—he wouldn't have wanted to miss that for the world. She was something else. Straight as a razor, but he had a hunch there was a naughty twin hidden inside.

He smirked, thinking how he'd love to be the one to find the key and unlock that door, letting the sexy siren out. He'd never met a woman so hot. The way she'd come with one flick of his tongue. Cripes, it made him stiff just thinking about it. If her reaction had been that strong, just imagine what he could do to her given the time.

He climbed into his Jeep, considered the possibility of turning up at her door and seeing if she'd let him in. But he remembered Kyle's words about being smitten, and how the love bug had got him, and he didn't want to take any chance that that could be true. He'd be better off to stay clear of this woman and find himself another playmate soon. Someone who'd never stepped into Serendipity Falls and never tasted that sweet spring water.

Still, he drove by Tara's place just the same. He parked across the street and could see her upstairs bedroom light turn on. Behind the sheer curtains at the window he could barely make out a form, but he could tell from her movements that she was getting undressed.

He should leave instead of staying here like some kind of sick voyeur. What if someone from the neighboring homes called the police, or went out for a walk and found him sitting here, staring at her bedroom window? The bad rep wouldn't do him or his business any damn good.

He started the engine then paused and looked up again. Tara stood at the window gazing out. He didn't think she saw him, but with the light behind her, he could see her clearly. She wore an old, white, LA Dodger T-shirt that did nothing to hide her curves.

She had a body, that's for sure. And after tasting it, it was damn hard to put out of his mind.

* * *

Tara had been ready to go to bed, but something made her glance out the window. She saw Devon's Jeep parked across the street. Her heart went into overdrive, and she put a hand on her chest to steady the pounding.

She remembered him touching her, his hand on her breast, hot mouth suckling her nipple. The sensations had been, well, sensational! Electrifying. Orgasmic. She'd wanted a lot more of it, that's for sure. But one of her big problems was that she had no patience. In anything. Relationships, her career, sex. Usually she just wanted to get it over with so she could do what she liked best—to cuddle. But with Devon--hell's bells--she'd come so quick she'd missed out on all the fun.

Damn. Now if she wanted it, she had to go to him and ask. Did he expect her to go outside and invite him in? He sure had some nerve! As if she'd lower herself to do that. No way. No matter how much he turned her on, she'd never, well, never was probably the wrong choice of words. It was extremely unlikely that she'd ask him for sex, but would wait instead for him to pursue her.

Which he would. If he wasn't interested, why would he be sitting outside, watching her window from his car? Huh? Simple conclusion. He wanted her as much as she did him. So, that being said, why didn't he just knock on her door and tell her how much he wanted to make love to her, maybe give her an example or two?

They both knew they weren't going to have a relationship. It was all about sex, but it would be good sex, she had no doubt. Her body started to hum, just thinking about it.

What had that drink been he'd given her tonight? A golden nipple. No, no, a slippery one. She wanted a slippery nipple all right. And she'd have one if he would only do what he wanted—come inside, take her into his arms, and make sweet love to her. She wanted him here, beside her, slipping his hand up her t-shirt, touching her in all the right places…and the wrong.

Perhaps, there really was another part of her dying to escape. Or was it the mountain air that stirred wants and needs deep inside, feelings she'd never known to exist? Her breath hitched, and she felt instant heat. My God but she wanted him. If he knocked on her door, she'd pull him in so fast he'd never stand a chance to retreat.

She watched him for a moment, hoping he'd feel her eyes on him, but then he started the car, and with a mixed sigh of regret and relief she waited until he drove away. Only then did she turn off the light, and slide under the duvet covers.

The following morning, she decided to go for a walk since she had an extra hour to kill. It was a lovely, brisk morning and she walked down the ploughed gravel road to town, discovering new streets and shops that she hadn't seen before. She went in search of a hair stylist, knowing she'd need one soon and a nail salon for her mani-pedis.

Unable to find either, she made a mental note to ask Cindy. Otherwise, she'd have to take a trip into Serendipity.

It had been amusing to see Cindy's reaction to Ken, and she wondered if they'd hooked up last night. Cindy didn't seem to share the same inhibitions as her, the lucky girl. She took whatever she needed, not afraid or ashamed to enjoy her pleasure and passion.

Tara wondered if that girl inside of her was more like Cindy. She hoped so. Maybe if she was lucky she'd meet this person too. Meanwhile, she had enough on her plate just being Tara Reynolds, executive pastry chef, and keeping Phillip off her back. Marc had saved her ass, and now, a day later, she was relieved that he'd been pleased. After all, getting fired would have been a bummer for her resume.

Besides, she had a good feeling about this place. There was a lot of energy in the stratosphere. And it had nothing, not one thing, to do with Devon. To prove it, she'd stay away from his bar, stay away from him, and concentrate on what she did best. Work.

When she got to the hotel, she threw herself into her job, effectively reining in her creative nature. She managed to stick to the budget and meal plan not only that day, but the following day too. She was settling into the swing of things and not in such a rush to put her signature stamp on everything carried out the kitchen door. She could be a team player, and it was time for her to take a step back and show that skill set too.

Finally, the weekend arrived and she had half of Saturday and all Sunday off.

She took a drive into Serendipity Falls to check out the mall. She discovered a full service salon for her hair and nails, had her nails taken care of, and booked an appointment for her trim and Henna in two weeks' time.

She wandered around the mall, picked up a few extra emergency lights at Home Depot and some pretty underwear at Macy's, then stopped to watch the skaters at the indoor ice-skating rink. After a few minutes she felt someone's eyes upon her.

Her skin tingled and she glanced around but didn't see anyone staring at her. Still, the feeling persisted and then she got a hot flush, making that rash on her chest flare. Weird. She still had the pin-prick above her left breast. Right near her heart. Could it be heart palpations? Was it an anxiety attack?

She sucked in a couple of deep breaths, releasing them slowly. She'd been thinking about taking a twirl around the rink but not now. Something odd was going on with her body—hot flashes, fevers, a racing heart. She should check out a doctor since she was in town.

Turning to leave, she found herself chest to chest with Devon.

"What are you doing here?" she asked. "Were you watching me?"

"No. I was heading toward Home Depot, but I ended up here. I didn't see you until you turned around and bumped right into me."

"You weren't watching? I could swear I felt someone's eyes on me."

"Well, it wasn't me. Not that I wouldn't have stared, you look awfully pretty today."

"Thank you," she said, flushing again, this time with pleasure. "That's nice of you to say."

"It's the truth." He grabbed her hand. "Hey, do you skate? Now that we're here, let's give it a whirl." When she shook her head, he coaxed some more. "Come on. It'll be fun."

"No, I probably shouldn't. I was thinking about finding a doctor. My heart's been beating too fast, and I'm getting hot flashes." She chewed her bottom lip. "I'm way too young for menopause. At least I hope I am. I want babies one day."

His eyes narrowed as he searched her face. "How do you feel right now?"

"Okay, I guess. It's gone."

"Good. Had me worried." He slipped an arm around her waist. "One skate, then I'll give you the name of the only doctor in town."

"You drive a hard bargain," she crinkled her nose, and smiled up at him when she said it.

He laughed. "I haven't skated in years, and I have a strong urge. Let's do it."

She gazed at him, thinking how handsome and charming he was--and how she wished she could be a little more like Cindy and just go for it. "But don't you have to go to Home Depot? I don't want to keep you. I'm sure you're busy."

"It can keep." He grabbed her hand and led her forward. "We'll just make a few turns, then go about our business. Humor me. Please?"

"Did you hear that?" She glanced around, searching the faces of the people gathered around the rink.

"What?" He stopped and looked around.

"It sounded like a high pitched giggle. And I definitely feel someone's eyes on me."

"You're a good looking woman." He shrugged. "You should be used to it."

"Well, whoever it is, I wish they would mind their own business." She glanced over her shoulder. "Maybe they will when they see us together."

He put his arm around her waist. "We can skate arm in arm. That should tell the guy something." He winced. "Ouch, what was that?"

"What?"

"I felt something. Oh, never mind. Come on, let's buy the tickets and get our skates."

Once they had skates on, Tara wondered what the heck she was doing. She didn't want a guy in her life--not right now--especially one who sent her blood pressure catapulting to dangerous levels and made her think about doing him every which way. So why did she agree to skate with him, continue to flirt, and grab onto him for life support as they stepped out onto the icy rink?

Her legs wobbled and her knees buckled so bad, she had no choice but to hang on tight. It had nothing to do with the fact that every time she glanced his way, her breathing got all mixed up, and she felt a huge pang of longing inside her aching chest.

Being around him made her yearn for things. Ever since her mother died, she'd been independent and strong. Her father had sunk into a black pit and she'd had to take care of him, the house, paying the bills, until he got back on his feet again. Her dad recently remarried a woman he'd met in Florida. She was free to do anything she liked and go anywhere she pleased, not having to answer to anyone.

She was living the life she wanted. The life she'd worked for. And she didn't want a man screwing with that. She glanced his way, and the tips of her skates dug into the ice, causing her to trip.

Devon pulled her up in the nick of time and held her steady against his chest. Even through the heavy jackets, she felt his heart beating wildly. She put her hand on his chest and smiled. "Thanks. You saved me."

His eyes stared into hers for several seconds. People circled around them, dashing by dangerously close but they didn't move. Finally, he spoke. "You didn't drink any spring water, did you?"

"No, but I am awfully thirsty."

He shook his head. "If you've had enough, we could go for a coffee or something stronger, but no water. You mustn't drink it."

"Why?" She tilted her head to look at him better. "Is there something wrong? Is the lake tainted? Is it an environmental hazard or something?"

He smiled. "No, it's worse than that. Don't ask me, because I don't really believe it, but I just think it's safer to stay clear."

"What in the world are you talking about?"

"Some kind of love bug." His face turned three shades of red. "Lots of weddings taking place in Serendipity Falls."

She hooted with laughter, which caused people to look their way. She linked her arm with his, and they skated off. "Love bug," she teased. "That's the funniest thing I ever heard. You actually believe it?" She giggled again. "Oh, I'm definitely going to have a bottle of that water now. I can hardly wait."

"Don't. I'm warning you." He led her to the edge of the rink and climbed out. "You don't want to be messing with it. Trust me."

She followed him. "Come on." She raised her eyes to his and licked her lips, teasing him with a wicked grin. "I'm so thirsty."

"Have a beer. I wouldn't even trust the ice around here."

Tara laughed again. "This is ridiculous." She put a hand on her hip and studied him. "How long have you been living in this area?"

"All my life."

"Well, look at you. You've managed to survive quite well. Not married. No prospects. Seems to be no problem for you."

"That's because I'm smart enough not to drink it straight. Mixed with scotch once in a while, but never straight up."

She shook her head, still grinning. "Thanks for the skate, big fella. You better run off to Home Depot, get what you came for, and get out of town while the getting's good. Me, I might take a ride to the falls and see Sue. Have an early dinner. Maybe a glass of wine and some water on the side." She ran her fingers up his arm. "You see. I like to live dangerously. And being bitten by a love bug doesn't sound all that bad. Preferable to the West Nile virus anyway."

He grabbed her hand. "First, I have someone I want you to meet. My sister, Mila. She runs Wedding Fever, a boutique here in the mall. She can set you straight if you don't believe me. There's a wedding a month in this small town and she's cashing in." He eyed her for a second. "Unless you really do want to settle down and get married, that is. Maybe you were just stringing me along with this 'I don't do a year' crap. Far as I know, you might have come to the mountains hoping to trap some poor sap."

"You're crazy, you know that?" She laughed, but his distrust of her hurt. How dare he think she wanted him, or any man for keeps! She was just having fun, in the sack and out of it, as he was. Two could play the game. All women didn't want to trade a successful career with doing laundry and car pools.

She gritted her teeth. "I have as much interest in marriage as you do. But okay, I'll meet your sister—just to see if she's as nutty as you are. Lead on."

The store was at the far end of the mall, near Macy's, and had an enticing window. It was glitzy, with feather boas and heart shaped balloons, an enormous bottle of champagne in a picnic basket, and other fun romantic stuff.

Mila was helping a happy couple when they walked in. The two young lovers were all over each other, and couldn't keep their hands to themselves. It was cute to watch, and Mila was delighted to show the lovebirds what they could spend their money on. She talked them into overnight invitations, a rushed order wedding cake, and helped them book a hotel for their soon-to-be nuptials. She also insisted the blushing bride-to-be should try on a wedding dress that had only just arrived.

During all this Tara watched her with amazement, thinking what a clever business lady she was, and how much she resembled her two brothers. She was tall and slim, with long, curly dark hair, a big smile and simply gorgeous.

When the future bride rushed off to the change room, Mila sighed and looked up. Her eyes widened, and her mouth popped open. "Devon! How long have you been standing there?" She smiled at Tara. "And you brought someone. My, my, what a surprise."

She came over and extended her hand. "Hi, I'm Mila."

"Tara Reynolds. It's nice to meet you."

"Don't get your hopes up, dear sister," Devon said quickly. "This is a friend of mine and she's new to this area. Told her not to drink the spring water, and about the myth of Serendipity Falls. She doesn't believe me. Thought you might be able to convince her how serious it is."

Tara grinned. "Your brother's a bit loony, isn't he?" She gave Mila a warm smile. "Cute store you have here. Must be doing well with all those weddings going on."

"It's hard to keep up--not that I'm complaining, but I run out of inventory as soon as it comes in." She gave Tara an appraising look. "I could use some help if you're looking for a job."

"No, I'm a pastry chef at the Cascade resort. But thanks for the offer."

"Too bad. I have a feeling that you and I could get along." She shrugged. "Well, if I ever get a day off, I'll come to the hotel and ask for you." She turned her head to glance at her brother, then back at her. "So what are you two doing in town?"

"I came here to get my nails done and make a hair appointment and ran into Devon."

"And I came to get some stuff from Home Depot and saw Tara hanging around the ice rink, looking like she wanted to skate."

"I did not," Tara said emphatically. "You dragged me onto that ice."

"Like hell I did."

Mila looked them over. "Oh, oh. You've got it, haven't you?"

Devon stopped arguing and flushed a deep color of red. "No fucking way."

"Don't swear in front of your sister," Tara admonished him. "You're always so grumpy." She glanced at Mila. "Is he normally like this?"

Mila looked from one red face to the other. "My dear brother—I only hope this is what I think it is. You found your match." She turned to Tara. "Not to worry--we have some very quick, easy plans to make all your dreams come true."

"You don't mean…no, it's not like that. We hardly know each other," Tara stammered. "Not even sure if we like each other."

"Oh, yes you do! And I'm thrilled. I really am. I never thought my darling brother would ever succumb."

"Go to hell," he said. "Come on Tara. Let's get out of here."

Mila laughed. "I'll see you both back here soon." She winked at Tara. "Welcome to the family."

CUPID

I'd been sitting next to Tara during the drive to Serendipity Falls, but of course she hadn't known I was there. She may have sensed my presence at the ice-skating rink because she turned around several times as if looking for someone. It was kind of cool the way I had Devon appear at exactly the right moment. I shouldn't be so smug about my match-making skills since I've had a hundred and eighty years to perfect them, but I get such a big kick out of it, and occasionally still amaze myself.

I didn't spend the entire time with my two new lovebirds, as I needed to check on a few of my other projects. I put a couple together a few years ago, and recently I heard through the grapevine that they were having problems at home. I left Tara and Devon at the rink so I could pay my squabbling pair a visit. By the time I left they were no longer arguing--he had taken his Viagra that I conveniently left out for him, and voila! Before I knew it, they were in bed, making love with perfect harmony. I expect this particular couple will continue to give me trouble now and then, but as long as they've got me around I know they will remain true to each other, and if not blissfully, at least, happy.

I had time to flit around and see some of my other success stories, and I will share this with you now—it does my heart good, and fills me with pride to see the happiness I bring to people. I should never whine and complain about the fact I get no respect, because they bring me as much joy as I bring them. My cup runneth over.

CHAPTER TEN

Tara laughed when Devon made a quick getaway, and she decided she might as well have that early dinner at the Falls instead of heading home and cooking for herself. When she got there, Sue was happy to see her and asked about Devon and her job.

"I love it. Everything's working out great. So far. And I just ran into Devon at the mall. He's got a sister who runs the Wedding Fever shop, and I met her too. Really a sweet girl, but she seemed to think we were an item, which we definitely are not!"

"You barely know the guy," Sue agreed. "Too soon for a romance, I'd say."

Tara waved a menu over her face as she felt a little warm. "I've seen him a couple of times in Mammoth, since his bar isn't far from my cabin. But that's it." Tara's blush deepened at the little white lie. But a girl had to have some secrets. "I have a beautiful little A-frame that is picture perfect, with a fab view of the snowcapped mountains." She rubbed her hands together. "I'm just so glad I left LA and came up here."

"Well, the mountain air seems to be agreeing with you. You look wonderful," Sue said, placing a glass of spring water on the table. "You're practically glowing. No wonder his sister jumped to the wrong conclusion. You look like a woman's who's either in love or pregnant." She glanced down at Tara's figure. "You're not, are you?"

She laughed. "Nope. Neither. But Devon said the strangest thing. He told me the spring water is tainted and warned me not to drink it. I thought he meant polluted, a health risk, but then he said no, that the locals say it contains a love bug." She raised the glass of water, moved it around, looking for anything suspicious. "Isn't that crazy?" Carefully, she put the glass down as if afraid a bug might literally jump up and bite her.

Sue's eyes sparkled, but she shook her head. "There are rumors, but I don't believe it either." She glanced around at the other patrons, and lowered her voice so they couldn't hear. "I moved here five years ago after a heart wrenching divorce. I've been working here, drinking gallons of that water, and I swear nothing has happened to me." She sighed. "I wish it would."

"Aw, Sue, I'm sure it will. Maybe you just don't look available. You know how some people have that married look, while other women's body language shouts out loud and clear 'Single Woman—come and get me.' I think it's like that."

Sue ran a hand through her tight curls. "What's a gal to do? Have a t-shirt made up, advertising that I'm available?" she grumbled.

"Maybe you should," Tara said lightly. "I'll franchise them."

"Enough about me," Sue replied. "What can I get you, honey?"

"A glass of Merlot, but first, I'm going to drink this water." Closing her eyes, she lifted the glass to her lips, tasted the water, let it roll around her mouth before swallowing. When it didn't make her feel anything special, she downed the rest. "There. I did it." She wiped her mouth. "Hell, what's the worst that can happen?"

Sue pulled a pencil out of her hair, and said, "You'll get bit instead of me. End up with that handsome husband, maybe some kids." She sighed. "Okay, enough about that. For dinner, we have a meatloaf special and a good vegetarian lasagna. Can't go wrong with either."

"I'll try the lasagna and the house salad. And that glass of Merlot."

"Good choice." The door opened, and Sue turned her head. "Well, lookie who's here. The guy we were just talking about. Coincidence, or is he following you?" She grinned and winked.

Devon sauntered over to the booth and sat down across from Tara. "Hi, Sue. I'll have what she's having. But skip the water."

Tara smiled at him. "Try the meatloaf. It's on special. And I'm having Merlot."

Devon nodded. "Sounds like a good choice." Sue left and he stretched his long legs out. Tara could feel his feet next to hers.

She nudged his toe with the tip of her boot. "Didn't expect to see you here. Thought your sister had scared you silly." Grinning, she leaned forward, putting her elbows on the table. "I liked her," she said, rolling her eyes, "but boy did she have the wrong idea about us."

"You can say that again. She sees romance everywhere and it's her business to sell it. Have to admit she's damn good at what she does."

"So, what are you doing here? Come to see me?" Tara watched the color rise up his neck and knew he had.

He faked a yawn. "Got my shopping done, and now I'm hungry. Besides, I'm not in any rush to get back." He glanced at the empty water glass and raised an eyebrow. "I hope that was soda."

"Nope. The real thing. Fresh spring water. Delicious."

He also leaned in, closing the distance between them. His face was inches from hers as he whispered, "You drank it after I warned you?"

"After I inspected it for love bugs." She smirked. "Not that I expected to find any. It tasted fine. Actually, it tasted wonderful." The smirk slid off her face, and she wondered if defying the town's legend had been such a good idea after all. "Mila doesn't believe it." She glanced at Devon hopefully. "Does she?"

"Says not, but who knows? Maybe secretly she hopes they do exist. I would think she'd want to get married and have a family of her own. Not right this minute of course. She's still young and is working hard. But eventually."

"So what do these love bugs look like? Have they got tiny bows and arrows?" Tara asked. "Ouch! What was that?"

"What?"

"I felt something. A shooting pain in my chest."

"You better see that doctor next time you're in town. You seem to have a lot of issues." He looked at her closely. "Damn. I sure hope you haven't been infected. Don't want you to give it to me."

"I'm sure I'm okay. Probably just stress from the move and the new job."

"You've moved around a lot. Ever felt this stress before?"

"No, now that you mention it." She rubbed her chest and frowned. "So saying it's real, how would bugs make people fall in love?"

"Not sure. It sounds ridiculous to me too. I've never known anyone who's ever seen one or been affected, so I think we're safe."

"Good. I've got too many things to do before I fall in love."

"Agreed."

They were silent for a few minutes as Sue arrived with their wine. They touched rims and drank deeply, not making eye contact.

"Still, a wedding a month is pretty wild, isn't it?" Tara twirled her wine in the glass, lost in thought. "Very strange."

"Love bugs aren't real," he said with some force.

"I know that." She drank more of her wine, wondering why the idea had him so hot under the collar. "Why are you afraid to fall in love? Don't you get tired of just stringing girls along?"

"I don't string anyone anywhere. I'm upfront about my needs." He took a slug of his wine, his gaze never leaving her face. "When I want something I go after it."

"You do?" She licked her lips and noticed his eyes were drawn to her mouth.

"Uh-huh." He rolled the remaining liquid around his glass. "You know that tip you left me?"

"Sure do." She ran a finger up and down the stem of her glass. "I was in a generous mood."

"It wasn't enough."

"What do you mean?" She glanced away from him, pretty sure she had an idea where this conversation was headed.

"I mean you still owe me." He lowered his voice and captured her complete attention. "We aren't even. Not even close."

"Why not? After all, you didn't have to work very hard for it." She shot him a look. "I can't believe you're even bringing this up. It's not very gentlemanly of you."

"I don't feel gentlemanly. I never do when you're around."

"And why is that, I wonder?"

"I have no idea. Nothing to do with microscopic love bugs, I'd bet the bar. But I want payment." He finished his wine, then put the glass down firmly. "Tonight."

"Tonight?" she squeaked, thinking of a million reasons why it wasn't a good idea, despite her perked libido. "I don't think so. I'm sure I'm going to be busy. Very busy, all night long."

"Doing what?"

"Don't you mean doing who," she said in a teasing voice.

"Not funny." He looked cross. "I don't know what it is you do to me, but I know that until I figure it out, I'm going to keep banging on your door every night."

"Oh, yeah? What if I call the police?"

"You wouldn't do that. I saw you last night at the window looking at me. I know what you were thinking."

"No, you don't." She toyed with the wine stem, wrapping the napkin around the base. "Okay. I'll bite. What was I thinking?"

"You wanted me to come in and take care of unfinished business."

"I did not." *How did had he known?* She folded her arms under her chest and gave him a defiant look.

"Then why are you blushing?"

"I feel hot again. What is it about this place?" She removed her jacket and pulled off her sweater, wearing only a thin t-shirt underneath.

He glanced at her breasts then back at her mouth. He leaned across the table and whispered, "I want to do you right now. Here. On this table."

Her mouth dropped open but no sound came out. Heat flooded inside and out. She fanned her face. "No fair. You can't talk like that."

"It's this place. I'm warning you." He touched her hand. "Maybe we should take our dinners to go?" He was about to wave Sue over, when she put her hand over his.

"Not a chance," she told him. "I'm safe here."

"You're not." His fingers climbed her bare arm. "You aren't safe anywhere from me."

"Devon. Stop that. You're scaring me." If being scared meant she'd be willing to strip naked and do him right now—well yeah, she was freaking terrified.

He grinned, a very wicked grin. "No, I'm not. I'm exciting you, and you like it."

"Why don't you find yourself a city girl to terrorize? Why me? I'm a local girl now and that puts me off-limits."

"Says who? Besides, you look like a city girl, you dress like a city girl, and you smell like a city girl. Hence, fair game."

"Stop looking at me like that." She glanced behind him and saw Sue bringing the plates. "Oh, good. Here comes the food."

"I have a better idea for dinner." His naughty look devoured her body. "Something more delectable."

"You're a pig," she said softly, just as Sue dropped the salads on the table.

"Everything all right here?" she asked.

"Right as rain," Devon said with a twinkle in his eye. "I was just trying to get to first base with our new friend."

Sue blushed and giggled. "Well, if she's got eyes in her head, that shouldn't be too much of a problem. If it is, here's my number. Call me, baby."

He laughed and Tara kicked his foot. "You are so crass."

"Eat your salad," he replied and picked up his fork. "And your lasagna. You're going to need a lot of stamina."

"Oh no, I don't." She glared at him but picked up her fork too. "You come banging on my door, you'll see what you get. A big fat nothing."

He licked his lips. "I'll take my chances."

"If you're a gambling man, you should put your money on a sure bet."

"Oh, I'm sure I can make you last a little longer. Perhaps even a full five minutes."

She sipped her wine, her eyes meeting his over the rim of the glass. "Five minutes, huh? What about you? Think you could go the distance?"

"I'd bet the farm on it." Then he turned his attention to the food, and she sat there, appetite gone. All she could do was watch his mouth, and imagine what pleasure it could bring.

Tara finished her salad and picked at her lasagna. Sue insisted on boxing it up so she could take it home. Devon paid for both their dinners and walked her to the car. "I don't have to be at the bar until seven," he told her. "Kyle's opening."

"You want to use up your five minutes of fame?"

He chuckled. "Sure. There's plenty more where that came from."

"You're really cocksure of yourself, aren't you?"

"I know one thing. You want me as much as I do you."

She didn't argue. What was the point?

"Okay. I'll see you at my place. But don't expect much."

She slid into the Mini and didn't wait for him to reach his Jeep. She got out of the parking lot and headed home like the devil was chasing her.

For all she knew, he was.

CHAPTER ELEVEN

It was going on six when Tara entered her cabin, and the afternoon light had disappeared. Wanting to create a more romantic mood, she lit a few candles, did a quick tidy up, then dashed into the bathroom. She brushed her teeth, her hair, and dabbed on some perfume, just as the knock on her door came loud and clear.

Grinning like a fool, she practically ran to let Devon in. She could feel her heart pounding with excitement. One look at his face, and oh my, she wished she hadn't drank that spring water. He looked delicious, devilish, and determined. Whether it was a love bug or Devon's considerable charms, one thing was for sure. She was going to be putty in his hands tonight. Soft and moldable, and perfectly compliant, she actually looked forward to surrendering her will. He could do anything he pleased, and she hoped he would.

She licked her lips in anticipation as he waltzed in the room, and tried to steady her breathing. Heart beating way too fast, she had that familiar tug low in her belly, a primitive carnal need that seemed to be disrupting her life lately, and begged to be appeased. Oh, yes, she looked forward to his five minutes of fame, and then some.

Devon put his hands on her hips, and backed her up slowly, one strong thigh at a time. Yummy! She stared at him, eyes wide, mouth open. Over eager, like a panting puppy, that's what she was. But he was so meltingly gorgeous, what was a poor person to do?

"Hey, beautiful. Hope I didn't keep you waiting too long," he said with a sexy, smug smile.

"Not at all," she said lightly, trying to rein in her emotions. It wouldn't do to let Devon know how she wanted to rip his clothes off, and lick every inch of his body. He already had a good opinion of his sexual prowess, without her feeding his ego. "I wouldn't have been surprised if you'd changed your mind," she said, glancing at him through lowered lashes. Her fingers stroked the back of his neck and threaded in his hair.

She could play sexy too.

"And why would I do a dumb thing like that?" He dropped his head and kissed her lips, taking his time. Perhaps he'd forgotten that he had to be at work in less than an hour. Should she remind him, so he could speed things up?

No. She wanted to play with him first.

She leaned back, and gave him a teasing smile. "Maybe that nasty old love bug can be transferred by kissing. I drink the water, and by osmosis you get the bug." She grinned. "That would sure mess with your plans."

"My plans right now are to satisfy you in ways you've only dreamed about." He nibbled on her neck and she squirmed with delight.

"What—in just a few minutes? Don't think so, buddy." She turned her head so he had better access to her neck. "I'm not always as easy as that first time. You'll have to work much harder. And faster. Times running out."

He grazed the lobe of her ear and gave it a little tug. Instant heat flared inside of her. "What are you doing?" she whispered, wide-eyed and breathless. "You nipped me."

"Love bite. Did you like it?" He did it again. "I want to take my time with you. Enjoy myself this time around." He licked her neck. "Kyle can handle things on his own, while I handle things right here."

She wrapped her hands around his neck as they stood chest to chest. "How do you plan on handling things?" She kissed his throat. "How long have you got?"

"I'm not on a tight schedule, so don't worry. I'm going to work you over first."

"Like hell, you will." She gave a short laugh and pretended to slip away, but he grabbed her arm and reeled her back in.

"So, do you want to introduce me to your bedroom or would you prefer I seduce you right here?"

She bit her bottom lip and considered. Eyes half closed, she leaned back and watched him. "Um…let's see. This is certainly interesting, but we might have more space in bed. Besides, what if someone can see in the windows?"

"They better not be peeping in, or they might see me do this." His hand reached for her ass and brought her forward so they were touching all the way down. She could feel how hard he was, and a soft thrill raced inside of her. She moaned, and he slid even closer, holding her exactly where he wanted her, moving in such a way that made her wet and warm.

His hand slid under her sweater and played with her nipple. "You like this, don't you?" He kissed her softly, almost teasingly.

"Oh, it's all right," she answered, as if her heart wasn't going crazy. As if her muscles weren't as weak as a kitten's; and she didn't need to cling to him to keep from falling to the floor.

He laughed and pulled her toward the staircase leading upstairs. "Come on, baby. We don't have all night."

She followed him up the stairs, more eager than she wanted to admit. He chucked his leather jacket, kicked off his shoes, and ripped his sweatshirt over his head. He stood there, chest bare, wearing only his low-riding, faded jeans and a sexy smile.

She bit her lip, just watching him, taking it all in. What a hunk of burning love. Hers. For all of the next five minutes.

"Your turn," he said. "Take it off."

"Isn't that your job?" She raised her arms, and he slipped her sweater over her head, tossing it to the floor. Her slacks went next. Then he lifted her and deposited her on the bed, and began to stroke her in all the right places. His kisses were warm and tender, his hands busy touching her everywhere at once. He unhooked her bra and took her breast in his mouth and she thought she might die from pleasure. She was so turned on she didn't know how she'd stand it.

His hand slid inside her panties and he slipped them down over her ankles.

"Now Devon. Hurry."

His eyes twinkled and his lips curved in a smile. "Undo me."

She did as he asked, and he was commando, wearing nothing underneath. His cock sprang free and she gasped. "Oh, my God."

Then she came.

"Oh crap, oh, crap." Tara hid her face and giggled.

* * *

"You've got to be kidding me, right?" Devon fell down next to her. "It's all over? That's it. I didn't even get to touch you properly," he complained.

"I know, I know, but you got your five minutes worth, didn't you?"

"Hardly." He glanced at his watch. "Damn. I really should leave in half an hour. You think you could get excited again?"

"Probably. I could try." She bit her lip and he could see tears weren't far away.

He took her hand and kissed it. "Don't worry. I'm not mad at you. I just don't know how we're ever going to get anywhere if you keep climaxing so fast."

Her cheeks flamed, but she reached out to stroke his face. "It is a problem, isn't it? You just get me so hot."

"Are you always like this?" He sat up on his side, his head supported by his hand. "Some women have a hard time climaxing at all. I love the fact you're so sexual."

"I'm not normally. It's either the water or it's you. Take your pick."

"I prefer option two." He ran a finger down her naked body, enjoying the sight and feel of her even if he couldn't quite close the deal. It wasn't her fault that she was so hot for him. Lots of girls had been, and he didn't want her to feel bad about it. Heck they could keep trying—that was half the fun.

Since she didn't seem to mind his touching her, he continued. "We could try later. After I finish work." He kissed her lips softly. "I could close at ten thirty, be here by eleven."

"No, not tonight." She yawned. "I'll be too tired. I have all day free tomorrow. Maybe we could give it another try then."

"I'm skiing tomorrow," he said, disappointed, but not giving up. "Hey, you want to ski?"

"I could do that. Yes, lets. I'm only a beginner, but you said you were good, so I'm sure I'll do fine." She kissed his chest, and then stomach. He sucked in a breath, hoping her mouth might find something else she liked better.

Her head came up. "I used to be a better lover," she said. "Don't know why I'm peaking so early." She shifted her body weight, half lying on top of him. His cock pushed against her belly, while his hand fondled her boob. His hopes grew just as his dick did.

"You're still hard," she said a little breathlessly, as he pulsed against her.

"Thought you'd never notice."

"I noticed all right. But I don't want to rush it. Do you?"

He wanted to say, sure, why not? And slip in quick before she changed her mind. But he knew that wasn't what she wanted to hear and it wasn't the proper thing to do. Even if his cock had a different idea, and kept waving at her, hoping she might take pity on him.

He kissed the top of her head, and disengaged himself. "We'll wait until tomorrow. Maybe the cold weather will dampen your libido and we'll get to close the deal." When she didn't respond, he lifted her chin and looked her in the eyes. "Just kidding, doll face."

"No, you weren't. It's the truth. I'm a lousy lay."

He laughed, then seeing her face, he was instantly contrite. "I'm sorry. I didn't mean to laugh. Besides, it's sexy to be hot."

"No, it's not." She pouted. "I'm having all the fun here, and you're not getting any."

"I'm not complaining. Just touching you is enough. Look at you, baby. I'm a lucky guy."

"Oh, Dev. You say the nicest things."

He was rock hard again and he inwardly groaned. He wanted to be a good guy and leave her be, but hell, he also wanted to get laid. "I could be late. Not real late, but a few minutes."

She finally touched him, and a shudder ran through him. She stroked him for a few seconds, then bent down and took him in her warm, wet mouth. Dear Jesus, that pretty mouth of hers was doing things to him, driving him damn near nuts. He wanted to get inside that sweet little...

She pushed off him and sat up. "Dev? I think we should try again."

"You do?" He kissed her softly. "Thank you, Lord."

She lay back down, and spread her legs, reaching out for him. "Slowly," she said with a smile. "I don't want to miss a thing."

He took a second to slip on a condom, then positioned his throbbing cock next to her warm center. She widened her legs a little more and wriggled her butt down to take him deep. His elbows cushioned his weight and he looked at her for one long second, then dove in. The moment he broke through, heat pulsed and the blood flowed to his cock, strong and powerful like a volcano about to blow. He fought to hold it back, but like any good volcano, when it was ready nothing could keep the lid on. He felt a hot gush explode right through him and knew he'd blown it. It was over before he even started.

"Fuck, fuck, fuck." He rolled off her and punched the pillow. "I frickin' can't believe this."

She giggled, and he wanted to throttle her. "Are you always this quick? You're as bad as me."

"No I'm not! I've never done that in my life." He slid out of bed and grabbed his jeans, hopping on one leg as he put them on. Once his fly was done, he turned around. "What the hell is going on?"

CUPID

When I got to the restaurant across from the Falls, I sat on the table next to the salt and pepper, right in front of Devon and Tara. I could tell from their conversation that they were happily flirting and making plans for a good time. I left with Devon, and when Tara let us in, I snuck up the stairs while the two conversed. I waited in the bedroom, resting my head on her pillow until I heard them enter the room and climb into bed. I skedaddled off the pillow just in time and took up a seat on the window sill, where I gazed at nothing but snow covered trees. Things were moving along nicely, or so I thought, but then suddenly everything went awry. Oh, how I hate it when that happens!

I do so want people to get along and learn to love each other. After all, what is more important than love? Nothing, I tell you. It warms the cockles of your heart, puts a smile on your face, and peace in your soul. Without it, there is no reason to get out of bed.

Speaking of bed, Tara and Devon seem to enjoy their time together. They laugh and smile and tease, and passion simmers underneath. They are so perfectly suited—even I can see that. Still it takes time with humans-- they are so reluctant to trust their emotions when it comes to love. Eventually they will come to realize that sex is only a small pleasure in discovering that special someone who makes your life complete. Important, maybe, but shadows in comparison to the many joys they encounter on the road to marital bliss.

CHAPTER TWELVE

Devon woke up early, determined to make today his day to finish the job he started with Tara. He wasn't sure why the sex thing wasn't working out, but there was no doubt that they were hot for each other. Too damn hot, that was the problem. He'd never exploded like that with any other woman. At least, not since he was sixteen.

Well, he'd have to make it up to her today. As soon as they finished skiing, before she had a chance to shower and warm up, he'd have her naked and in his bed. All he had to do was get through a few hours of skiing, bring her home while Kyle was still out, and bababa-zing. He'd be in and out before she had a chance to tremble.

It wasn't the way he liked to do things, but she gave him no choice.

She thought they were both lousy lovers, but he'd prove her wrong. He would come, she would come, then they'd go for a nice dinner. It would be a superlative day.

Superlative—he couldn't recall ever using that word before. Fucking great was more to his liking. Okay, they would have a fucking great day.

Satisfied with his decision, he took a shower then made a big, hearty breakfast. Eggs, bacon, whole wheat toast, the whole nine yards. He would need his stamina for what he had planned. He was a good lover—maybe too good if Tara's reaction was any indication of his sexual prowess. And one moment of blowing his load, didn't mean a hill of beans when you took into account the number of times he'd pleasured a woman in his life. So he wasn't worried about his lack of control. Not at all. It was Tara who got over heated, and that made him hot. He'd better skip his favorite aftershave because that might trickle a reaction in her. Or kiss her too much. Shouldn't compliment her either. No touching of the boobs, no touching down under. Hell, exactly what could he do to get into her pants?

This wasn't going to be as easy as he first thought. It might need some careful planning. Perhaps he could tie her up. No, she'd probably like that. He'd handcuff himself. Naw, that was too weird. What the fuck could he do so she wouldn't go off again? He'd never had this problem before, and as much as it flattered his ego, he wasn't sure he liked it.

He wished he had some trusty friend to ask for advice, but his brother was closer to him than anybody, and he sure didn't want to discuss Tara with him. His sister might be able to shed some light on the matter from a female point of view, but that was so not going to happen. He couldn't discuss Tara with anyone. If other guys knew she was such hot stuff they might want a piece of her. Over his dead body. She was his, even if he couldn't have her.

He gave himself a mental shake. What was he thinking? He didn't do relationships. Hell, no. For one thing, he couldn't afford a wife. He could barely afford to pay the taxes and upkeep on the cabin, and keep the business alive. It was a hard task balancing the books each month, and Kyle had a bad habit of letting money slide through his fingers. Someone had to hold things together and that someone was him.

Besides, he liked casual, no strings sex. No one got hurt, and he didn't need all that romancy shit. He'd been in love once, engaged too. But after his accident, Nadine didn't bother to stick around, not when he woke up from his coma and had a head injury and all. He didn't blame her. He'd been like a baby, having to relearn stuff from scratch, and he didn't know if or when he'd completely recover, so why would a beautiful girl like that stick around?

No, it was better that she'd left. He'd had to work hard and hadn't needed any distractions, like a gorgeous clingy wife. Luckily, he'd recovered faster than expected, and his mental capacity hadn't suffered either. He was about as smart today as he'd been before the accident, but that's not saying much.

Still, he was smart enough to know he needed to watch his step and not let his little head over-rule the big one when it came to Tara. It was only sex. He intended to keep it that way.

Love-bug. Hum-bug!

* * *

They met outside the Main Lodge at the base of the mountain, taking the gondola directly to the summit. The place was crowded--as it should be at ten a.m. on a Sunday morning, two weeks into the season. Tara carried her skis over her shoulder, and with her free hand, she gave him a wave, smiling broadly, obviously looking forward to her ski lesson.

Which was just one of the little things he intended to teach her.

"Hey! I bought a winter pass so I can do this every weekend," she said happily. "What a beautiful day. Aren't we lucky?"

"Sure are." He intended to get luckier if things worked out. "It's always a good day on the mountain, but the sun is shining, the temperature above freezing, and there's a beautiful young lady smiling at me. What can possibly be better?"

"Last night could have been." She bumped his shoulder and grinned. "You were certainly in a rush."

"Ha-ha. Very funny. I had to go to work, remember?"

"Sure thing." Her eyes twinkled. "Glad you weren't late."

His ego was slightly bruised, so he raised a brow and gave her a pointed look. "Yeah, well, you came a little early too. If I recall."

She tossed her head and shrugged, looking a tiny bit smug. "True. I started it, and you followed suit."

He wanted to kiss away her smugness and show her that she wasn't in control as much as she liked to think. Instead, he leaned in and whispered, "I have plenty of ideas for later. Mutual satisfaction, baby." He wagged his brow and gave her a naughty boy smile. "But right now let's keep our minds on skiing." They stood in the gondola line which moved along quickly. "We're going to the summit where there are plenty of runs to choose from."

"The top of the mountain?" she asked, wrinkling her nose.

"Uh-huh, but don't worry. The terrain has something for all levels of skiers. I figured we'd try a few green runs, and then, if you're up to it, we might do a few blue. Groomed, of course."

She nodded bravely. "Sounds like a plan, but don't expect much. I skied a little while in college but that was several years ago."

"No problem. We'll take it slow." He assisted her with her skis as they clamored inside the gondola. They stood next to a window and watched the village drop away. It was an awe-inspiring view that he never quite got used to. How some people could work in an office or bake cakes all day, he had no idea--not when this glory lay before them.

"Pretty, isn't it?" he asked softly, placing a hand on her shoulder.

"It's gorgeous," she admitted. "You sure we shouldn't ski at a midway point? I might be a little rusty. Don't want to break anything."

"Don't worry." He dropped his head to whisper, and allowed his lips to graze her cheek. "I won't let anything happen to you. We'll start with a few short runs, let you get a feel for the skies, then ride one of the quads back up."

She turned and because of the close proximity she had to tilt her head back to look into his eyes. "You wouldn't be trying to get even, would you?"

"Even? What kind of guy do you take me for?"

"Just thought you might be punishing me." Her eyes danced and he knew she was teasing. "For last night."

"I can think of a better way." He kissed her cold nose, and wished he could taste her lips. But not in a crowded gondola. He wanted her alone. Alone and naked, withering beneath him.

She smiled, her eyes bright. "Me too." The gondola lurched as it came to a stop, and Devon grabbed her shoulders to steady her against him. "Here we go. Exit to the right."

He followed her out, and then led her away from the crowd to put on their skis.

She bent over to straighten her skies and her pretty little tush, tightly clad in black ski pants, drew his eyes like a magnet. He sucked in a breath of cold air, and forced his wicked thoughts away.

"Okay, how much do you remember?" He noticed his voice seemed unusually high pitched. "You know how to stop, right? If you start gathering too much speed, try to turn. If that doesn't work, let yourself go down. I'll be there to help you back up."

"Okay. I'm not a pretty skier, but I can usually stay on my feet."

"Good. We'll see how you do. I'll ski down thirty, forty feet or so, and then watch you come down." It was certainly safer than watching her cute behind. Eyes glued there, he could ski off a cliff.

"Show me the way," she said, and adjusted her ear muffs.

He pushed off, doing big winding turns, carving a route for her to follow. He turned and planted his poles, indicating that it was her turn. She grinned and waved with her pole, then began her downhill descent. She didn't follow his carved route, but went straight down, making tight turns, and whizzed on by him.

When he finally caught up to her, she burst out laughing.

"You should have seen your face!" she sputtered. "I had you fooled, didn't I?"

"So you're an expert now?"

"No, hardly. But I can ski the easy slopes well enough. It's the trickier ones that give me a problem."

He frowned. "You could have told me."

"What? And spoil all the fun?" She bumped into him, trying to make him fall. "Besides, I only look good on the green. My legs are all over the place if I get on a steep hill... and forget moguls. They kill me."

"I have half a mind to do just that." He gave her arm a playful push. "Okay, show off. You go first and I'll follow. Now that I know you can handle yourself, this will give me something nice to look at."

She stuck out her tongue. "There you go again. Always checking out my butt."

"It's worth a look or two."

She pushed off, and Devon skied right behind her, enjoying the view more than ever. By lunchtime, they'd skied half a dozen runs and decided to take a short break. They ate at the Summit and found a table with a panoramic vista view. It was truly breath-taking, but no more so, Devon thought, than the woman sitting opposite him.

"Why are you staring at me?"

"I don't know. You just continue to surprise me."

"In a good way or a bad?" she asked, tilting her sunglasses to see him better.

"Mostly good." He winked. "The bad we still have to work on..."

She glanced away. "Perhaps we shouldn't."

"What do you mean?" He nudged her ski boot with his own, but she ignored it.

"Well, we might be better friends than lovers. Neither of us wants to get romantically involved. And sex messes things up between friends." She licked her dry lips. "So what are we doing?"

"Having a good time?" he answered, wondering what had flown up her butt.

She shook her head, staring straight ahead. "We should leave well enough alone." She sighed. "After you left, I did some thinking. You and me and sex--it doesn't make sense."

"Neither does being friends. I enjoy being with you, and yes, I want more. Don't you?" When she didn't answer, he added, "I don't want to be with anyone else."

"Ditto, all of that. But can't we leave out the sex part? We can't seem to get it right. Maybe that's telling us something."

"We need more practice, that's all." He laced his fingers through hers, noting how chilled they were. He put her small hands to his lips and breathed to warm them. "Besides, you're up one. You want to quit now?"

"What? You're keeping score? This isn't a poker game, you know."

He let his gaze roam slowly over her face and saw the warmth creep into her cheeks. "Come on. Once more. For me." He gave her his best sexy smile.

"What if I say no?" She lifted her chin and looked into the distance.

"You'd have to find your own way down to the main lodge." He looked at the multiple runs heading off in every direction. "Good luck with that."

She smacked his arm. "You're a pig. And you wouldn't leave me. Would you?"

He grinned. "Not likely, but if I were you, I'd say yes and not have to find out."

"Instead of sex, can't I just make you a pie or something? You must have a favorite."

"Oh, I do." He chuckled. "Warm apple pie and I know exactly where I want to eat it."

She didn't need to ask.

CHAPTER THIRTEEN

They skied down the mountain, a long, slow ski which became a little slushy nearing the bottom, but Devon was proud of how well she did and that her legs held out.

He might have to give her a reward for that.

"What are you smiling about?" she wanted to know.

"My little secret." He ruffled the top of her head. "You did good up there. Nice work."

"Thanks. I really enjoyed it!" Her enthusiasm spilled over, bubbling out like a warm Crème Brulee. "It was exciting to be up on skis again. So much fun! Thank you, Dev."

"You've very welcome, Tara." He chucked her chin. "Don't think that's going to get you out of it."

"Out of what?" she asked innocently.

"You know what. And I'm ready for it now."

"Now?" she squealed. "I didn't agree to anything and besides, it's not even dark. On top of that, I need to rest. That was a lot of exercise in one day. More than I've had in years."

"Yes, well, I think I might prefer you tired. Not too worked up."

"Oh, that's just not fair!" she sputtered. "How insulting can you get?"

"Oh, there's plenty more where that came from."

"You're impossible. And for the record, I didn't say yes to sex. All I said was I'd bake a pie."

"Forget the pie and rest. I recommend we both take a nice long nap."

"Together? I don't think so. Besides baking relaxes me." She worked a couple of kinks out of her neck. "Give me a couple of hours and then come over. I'll cook dinner, and you can have your pie."

His lips twitched. "I like the sound of that."

"I bet you do." She unzipped her jacket and stuffed her gloves inside the pockets. "Come around five. That should give me enough time."

"I'll bring wine. Want me to pick up anything else?"

"No. Do you like beef bourguignon?"

"Think so. It's a stew, right?"

"A very delicious stew. I use good beef, a little cognac, and nice red wine."

"Sounds great, but don't go to too much trouble." Then, as an afterthought, he added, "Forget I said that. Knock yourself out."

She laughed. "Sheesh. How did I ever get mixed up with the likes of you?"

"You just got lucky. Twice," he said to tease her.

"Go away. I'll see you at five."

Devon gave her a mock salute and headed to his locker. Since he was in the ski patrol, he kept his skis and gear at the lodge. Then he found his car in the crowded lot and headed home.

Kyle was lying on the sofa when Devon waltzed in the door.

"Hey," Kyle said in way of greeting, turning his rapt attention to whatever he was watching on TV.

"Hey, yourself. Didn't you ski today?" he asked. "It was something else."

"Figured I'd go later," Kyle muttered. "I hate the morning crowd."

"Wasn't too bad. Another month from now the lineups will be twice as long."

"I know. Bad for skiing, good for business." Kyle stretched and yawned. "What do you want to do for dinner? Pizza? Chinese?"

"Not tonight." Devon grabbed a beer from the fridge. "Tara invited me for dinner."

"That's cool. You should taste what you're getting, since marriages around here are longer than a life sentence." He added, "You guys should really think about getting those invitations in the mail."

"Ha. Ha. Very funny." Devon threw a pillow at his younger brother. "Where's Lisa? Working today?"

"Yeah, she's got a full schedule every weekend."

"That's good. It pays the rent." Which is a lot more than we've been doing lately on our business venture, he thought to himself.

"Uh-huh, but it kinda sucks that I have Sunday off and she's at work."

"Whoa, bro. Now who's the one who's got it bad?" Devon popped the lid and took a long swill of the ice cold brew, then sat down on an overstuffed chair, his legs dangling over the arm. "What happened to the three date rule? Three dates and you're in, then you're out."

"It didn't feel right with Lisa."

"Yeah. I know what you mean." He closed his eyes for a moment, thinking about Tara. There was something about her—he couldn't put his finger on it, but she got to him. More than any other woman had in the past several years. She was fresh, fun, exciting. He liked her company, and that in itself was unusual. Normally, he looked forward to his date, knowing he'd be between her thighs by the night's end, and then he was happy to drop her home. It wasn't like that with Tara. Whether he scored or not, he still enjoyed being with her.

He couldn't blame it on the water either. Tara was just the kind of woman he'd want in his life if he ever had the urge, which he didn't. Not only couldn't he afford to take on a wife, but it would be too demanding. The few hours of freedom he had between ski patrol and running the bar were his to do with as he wanted, and he liked it that way. He made no bones about it—he was nothing but a broken down, old ski bum with no plans to change.

Now, a girl like Tara would set her sights on someone with a bigger future than him and rightfully so. He'd back away soon before either of them got in too deep.

But first he needed one last chance to even the score.

* * *

The smell of freshly baked apple pie greeted him the moment Tara opened the door. His mouth watered as he sniffed the air. "Oh, wow, does that smell good." He put his arms around her and pretended to sniff her too. "Is that you I smell?"

"It better not be," she laughed. Pulling him into the kitchen, she lifted the lid off the pot on the stove. "Take a whiff of this."

Tender beef, carrots, onions, mushrooms, garlic, and wine simmered on the top of the stove. "Beef Bourguignon," she said proudly. "And you'll never taste a better one."

"Looks delicious." He picked up the ladle and was about to sneak a taste, when she snatched it away.

"Be patient. It needs another half hour."

"Thirty minutes." He glanced at his watch. "You want to work up an appetite?"

She shook her head, but smiled. "No, I do not. Can't you think of anything else besides sex?"

"Sure. I can think about food, wine, and kissing you senseless. Sex would be a plus, but it's not necessary."

"Really?" She gave him a speculative glance. "That's so sweet."

He shrugged. "It's true. Although, I could be persuaded." He glanced down, the bulge chaffing at his jeans. "This guy's already getting excited."

Her cheeks flushed. "Go open the wine. Make yourself useful. I promised you pie. Nothing else."

He raised an eyebrow. "And you know exactly where I want to eat it."

"Give it a rest already. I really want us to be friends. Can't we be friends?"

"Sure." He put his hands in the air, a sign of surrender. "If you don't want me in your bed, I'm fine with that. You just say the word."

Stepping away, he busied himself with opening the wine. She stood staring at him, her expression unreadable.

"Deal," she said slowly. "I'll think about it and let you know." She began to stir the pot with a little more gusto than necessary, and he waited until she'd finished to hand her a glass of wine.

He toasted her. "Thanks for inviting me to a home cooked dinner."

"I like cooking for someone other than myself. There doesn't seem to be any point to it when I'm alone."

"No problem. Whenever you feel the need to feed someone, Kyle and I are only a phone call away."

"Oh! I never thought about inviting him. Give him a call if it's not too late."

"He's busy," Devon told her, putting his wine glass down. "Besides, your stew looks too good to share." He came up behind her and put his arms around her middle. Sniffed over her shoulder. "Smells great too."

She laughed and pushed him away. "You must be hungry. Go sit down and let me finish up here. I don't want you distracting me."

She put a loaf of sourdough bread in the oven, then leaned back to sip her wine. "You've lived here a long time, Devon. How come some girl hasn't hooked you yet?"

"I was engaged once but that didn't work out." He rolled the stem of the glass around in his fingers, watching the red wine swirl in the glass. "After my

134

accident I had a lot of work to do to get back on my feet, and then a few years later another tragedy hit. Our grandparents were in Greece, celebrating their 50th wedding anniversary, and their bus went off a cliff. It's just been one bad thing after another."

"Good God, yes," she murmured.

He glanced up, and her eyes were on him. "After that, Kyle and I bought this business and we're barely scratching out a living. There's just no time for a woman." He added as a warning, "Can't see it happening anytime soon, either."

"I guess not." She reached out a hand to touch his arm. "I'm so sorry about your grandparents. What a terrible thing to happen. Were you close?"

He nodded. "Very. Grams and Pops were the best." He felt himself getting choked just talking about them, but he knew she'd have more questions. People always did.

"Were they your mom's parents or your dad's?" she asked gently.

"Mom's. But we all loved them very much." He looked away. "Pops and Grams lived in San Francisco and had a house on the bay. We spent a lot of time in the summer out on their boat, and they kept us kids for weeks at a time. They were an extended part of our family."

Tara wrapped her arms around him and gave him a kiss. There were tears in her eyes.

He disengaged himself, wanting to finish this conversation and be done with it. "Mom took it really hard. They sold their business soon after and moved to Maui."

"That must have been hard on you too. Having your parents move away." She looked at him as if seeing someone new. Someone she understood.

He put on his poker face, not wanting anyone to get too close. He protected his privacy and respected it in others. "Mom was heading for a breakdown, and the change has done her a world of good."

"I'm glad. Do you visit often?"

"In the summer things are slow around here. Kyle and I closed the bar for a couple of weeks in July and flew over. Learned to surf too."

She smiled. "I bet you did. So who was better? You or Kyle?"

He lifted a brow. "Who do you think?"

"You, of course." She pecked his cheek. "I'm sorry for all the bad things that happened. You're a great guy."

He shrugged and stepped away, determined to steer the conversation in another direction. One that didn't involve pity. "A lot of people think I'm a real bastard. I probably am."

She was silent for a few minutes, just stood there looking at him. "Okay. Just a few more questions, then we'll eat."

"Shoot. Ask me anything you like."

"Okay." She folded her arms. "What about Ken, the realtor. He says you broke his sister's heart."

"Ken's a jerk," he said without bitterness. "Besides, she came after me. I tried to warn her, but she didn't want to hear it."

"That's not how he tells it."

"He shouldn't be telling it at all." Devon shook his head, then rubbed his jaw. "She was just a kid, and I kept telling her that, but she insisted she knew what she was doing." He pushed the wine glass away. "Seems I was wrong."

"Why? What happened?"

"Do you really want to know this stuff?"

"Yeah." She sat down at the table, and played with the silverware. "I really do."

"Okay, but I'm not proud of it."

"Doesn't matter. I want to know why Ken has it in for you. I think I know you well enough to say you're a good person."

He gave a grim smile. "All right. Here's the truth-- the way I see it, anyway." He sucked in a breath. "One night, she came to the bar and wouldn't leave. I ended up driving her home. Since she couldn't walk I helped her inside and laid her down on the couch. She grabbed me and pulled me down. Guess I didn't fight very hard."

"Ken said you dated her for a couple of weeks and then never called her again."

"That's not true. I didn't date her at all. It was just that one night, and I guess it meant a lot more to her than it did to me."

She seemed to mull that over. "I feel bad for her, but I believe you."

"Good. Let that be the end of it then."

"I will. I'm not thinking of her, but about us." She reached out a hand and touched his arm. "Way I see it, we've started our relationship, or whatever it is, on the wrong foot. Should have gotten to know each other properly before hopping in bed together. Obviously, that didn't work for us, so maybe we should take a step back and let nature take its course." She let that sink in, then said softly, "there's a lot about you to like, and what's the harm in taking this one day at a time?"

"I think we are." He took a slug of wine. "Yesterday we ice skated. Today, we skied. Not like we're getting engaged or anything."

She laughed. "Of course not, but I'm thinking of the bedroom. Let's slow things down. Okay?"

He cupped her face and looked into her eyes. "Not as much fun, but if that's what you really want, then yes. We could do that."

She turned around and pulled the loaf of bread out of the oven, giving him a birds-eye view of her rounded ass. His mind might agree with her, but other parts of his anatomy had different ideas.

CHAPTER FOURTEEN

Tara had tossed a salad, and she served that with the stew and warm bread. They sipped on the expensive bottle of French wine and listened to Andrea Bocceli as background noise.

"You like opera?" she asked.

"Not really. But I like this. Who is it?" Devon asked and refilled both their glasses.

She told him. "He's blind, and he's amazing. I saw him perform once in Vegas, and it was one of the best performances I've ever seen. So much passion and soul. I can feel his music in my bones."

He smiled. "I love your enthusiasm. Everything excites you."

She blinked and took a quick sip of her wine. They were actually having a meaningful conversation. She liked that. "What about you? You're still passionate about skiing. That's something. What else do you get excited about? And please, don't say me."

He glanced at the fire, avoiding her eyes. "I don't know. Nothing much. I wanted something once but that didn't work out. Now, I don't want for anything."

"That's sad."

"No, it's not. It's practical. Less disappointment that way."

"Dev, that is really, really sad." She jumped out of her seat and came around the table to give him a hug. "I can't imagine not wanting anything or not being excited about everything." She kissed his cheek and draped her arms around his neck. "I lost my mom too, but that didn't temper my eagerness to live and be all that I can be. My mom would have wanted that."

Devon kissed the palms of her hands. "I want you. That's something."

She shook her head. "No, it's not," she said with disappointment. "It's just sex." She pulled her hands away and returned to her seat. "Finish eating and then you can have pie."

"Like a good little kitty," he said with a twinkle in his eye. "Meow, meow, meow."

"I'm surprised you remember that nursery rhyme." She took a bite of the stew. "This is fabulous, if I do say so myself."

"It is and so are you."

She put her fork down, feeling out of sorts. All he wanted was sex, and she wasn't sure what she wanted, but perhaps one step deeper. "Don't look at me that way and don't say nice things either. I want to know the real you, not the shallow person you pretend to be."

"Shallow? This is as good as it gets." He took a large mouthful, then picked up a piece of bread to dip in his bowl. "Why don't you tell me about yourself? How many hearts have you broken?"

"None that I know of. Last guy I dated turned out to be married. Jerk. He broke my heart, not the other way around."

"Well, you can't blame him exactly. No matter how perfect his wife was, when he met you it would have been game over. A guy would need to be a eunuch not to feel an itch with you around."

She tried to hide her smile but it wasn't easy. He just made her feel so darn good.

They ate as much as they could, careful to leave a little room for the freshly baked pie that sat on the counter. She'd left it there as a visual reminder, although the scent of the apples and cinnamon still lingered.

They took their coffee into the living room and sat down in front of the fire, resting between courses. She snuggled close to Devon and wondered what it would be like to have a permanent home and a family of her own. For the past ten years, she'd worked hard to free herself from the memories of being trapped, the years of wanting to escape to some place light and happy, where sickness and death didn't exist.

She rested her head on his shoulder, and he kissed the top of her head. "That was a wonderful dinner. Can't remember when I last had a meal that good."

She lifted her head and kissed his chin. "You're welcome. Next time, I'll invite Kyle too."

"You don't need to do that." His arm was on the back of the sofa, his hand on her shoulder, fingertips lingering on the side of her breast. "I want you all to myself. He's got a girlfriend anyway."

"Then I could have them both over."

"What's wrong with just me?"

"Nothing's wrong with just you. I like everything about you. Even the fact that your hand is straying toward my boob."

He laughed. "I'm glad you don't have a problem with that." He bent his head to kiss her. They kissed for a long time, and she felt heated, with a growing yearning in her belly. A yearning she didn't want to have. Taking it slow was the right plan. She had made enough mistakes, and she didn't want any more disappointments, bruises to the heart, or useless tears. Never again.

She pushed him away. "You're a wonderful kisser. I might be a good cook, but you excel at kissing." Her eyes swept over his handsome face. "I like you enough to stop this from going any further."

"Why don't you stop thinking so much, and just do what feels right?"

"You're talking about sex again! I thought we agreed to give it a rest?"

"I agreed to please you, but I can think of a better way."

"Yeah, right." She rolled her eyes. "Here we go again. Only this time I can't come, isn't that the deal?"

He chuckled and lightly caressed her breast. The back of his fingers brushed her nipples which instantly tightened and swelled. "I didn't say you couldn't come, I just suggested that perhaps you could wait a little longer. Don't worry, you'll get your chance before the night is through."

She stopped his hand from moving, not wanting to be further aroused. "Doesn't sound like a whole lot of fun for me. I think we should cool our jets, and have dessert."

"How about one kiss first?" He nuzzled her neck, which sent shock waves right through her. How could she resist when everything he did had her over the edge?

"What's wrong with waiting?" she asked grumpily, knowing she was losing the battle of wills.

"We'd get here eventually, so why waste the time?" His mouth was doing strange, wonderful things to her insides, heating her from the tips of her toes to the roots of her hair. He slipped his hand under her sweater and cupped her breast. In spite of herself she moaned, and leaned further into him. She undid a couple of buttons on his shirt to stroke his fine chest hair. She kissed his neck, and nibbled on his ear.

"Are you ready?" he asked, his voice a husky whisper.

She sighed, knowing she wanted it too. "Okay, if you really think we should do this, I'll be a sport. Go ahead. Give it your best shot."

"How perfectly romantic," he said dryly.

"You don't want romance, remember? You just want to get laid." She led the way upstairs. "Here's the deal. I'll make an effort to restrain myself, but you better not take all day about it. I want a little satisfaction too."

"I won't." He pulled her down on the bed, and began to undress her. "I promise."

He took off her sweater, and kissed the lacy cups of her bra, pulling it down to expose her nipples. He took one in his mouth, and rolled it between his teeth. She moaned her pleasure. Unhooking her bra, he pushed it aside, and blew a warm breath on each one, sending ripples of excitement shooting right through her. "Oh, I like that," she murmured, holding his head.

He lowered his mouth and grazed her stomach, then went lower still. Slipping a finger into her lacy pants, he found her wet and kissed her hard.

"Hold on, while I get the condom out of my pants."

"Hurry up. You know I'm not good at waiting."

"Yeah. No need to remind me." He jumped up off the bed, ripped open the packet with his teeth, dropped his jeans and jockey shorts to the floor, and leaned over her.

"Can you help me with this?"

She smiled. "Give it to me." His erection was only inches from her mouth and she wanted to taste him first. She let her tongue roll over him and took him deep. He shuddered, and for a second she thought that might be it, but then he pulled back and grabbed the condom, eager to get it on.

"Shit!"

Her eyes flew open. "What?"

"Ripped the fucking thing."

"You've got to be kidding. You got another one?"

"Thought I did, but the package is empty. How about you?"

"I just moved here. I have no need."

"Well, you do right now."

"Can't you just run to the store or something?"

"Shit, shit, shit." He pulled his jeans back on. "Don't go anywhere. Don't move. I'll be back in ten minutes."

"Hurry! Don't be long." She touched his naked chest. "I want you too."

He kissed her quick and hard. "I'll be back, sweetheart. Keep the fire burning."

She watched him leave, then got out of bed. She finished undressing and decided to put on a sexy nightie, then slipped back between the sheets. Her body was humming and she hoped he'd be back soon before she lost the urge.

She closed her eyes, thinking of how magnificent he'd looked standing naked over her. She thought about her mouth on him, how he'd tasted, and how much she wanted to please him.

She waited, counting the seconds go by. She sighed, and yawned. Then yawned again.

* * *

Devon stopped at the closest drug-store, bought several packages and rushed back to Tara's. He'd been gone less than twenty minutes.

He entered the bedroom, and kicked off his pants and shirt. The light was off, and Tara lay on her side. He snuck under the covers and kissed her ear. His hand swept around to cover her breast. He whispered, "Honey, I'm home."

She answered with a snore.

He lay there for several minutes, debating whether he should wake her. Gently, patiently, he fondled her breasts, hoping she'd stir and turn to him. Nada.

He slipped a hand down to her thighs and lifted the hemline of her nightgown. He touched the silky short curls which hid her womanly delights and rested his hand against the soft, heat of her. Still no response.

He waited for a few seconds more, but as he listened to her soft snores he felt his hard-on wither away. Devon got out of bed, put his clothes back on, and headed downstairs. He had one hand on the door when he remembered the pie she'd baked for him. He cut two large slices, wrapped cellophane over them, and left by the side door.

He'd been promised pie, not sex, and a luckless ski-bum like him would take what he could get.

* * *

The sound of the door closing woke Tara. She lifted her head off the pillow and looked around for Devon. He wasn't in bed with her, and she could see from the light in the bathroom that he wasn't there either.

"Dev? Are you downstairs?" she called as she slipped out of bed. She tiptoed down the stairs, and called his name again. She saw the pie had been cut into and looked out the window to see Devon's Jeep disappearing down the road.

What the hell! So what if she'd fallen asleep for a few minutes? She blinked away tears. Why hadn't he woken her? She rubbed her chest, feeling a burning pain. Men! Didn't she know any better? All she ever got for her troubles was a wounded heart.

Devon was just as bad as the rest, maybe even slightly worse. He was quick to admit that he didn't want anything more than a roll in the sack. Didn't even pretend otherwise. Sheesh—what was she thinking? Why not just wear a big fat sign on her chest, saying "stab me now."

From now on, no more casual sex. Especially with Devon. All he wanted was a fucking good time. She picked up the pie and tossed it in the bin. Well, he wouldn't be getting it from her. That's for damn sure. She turned off the lights, except a small lamp near the window, then double locked all her doors. She returned to her bedroom, now unable to sleep.

Why was she disappointed? What had she expected? He'd been upfront with her, so if she'd wanted a little more than he could give, he was not to blame. She was smart enough to know that good looking guys took what they wanted, when they wanted, and a woman had to be on her toes.

It was time for her to be a little more like Cindy. She didn't need to fall in love with every Tom, Dick, or Harry willing to show her a good time. Hell no. Two could play this game. And if she wanted to climax, she could do that too. Show restraint—I don't think so buddy!

CHAPTER FIFTEEN

The first snowstorm of the season was nearly forgotten as the temperature warmed and a mild rain washed the snow away. The roads and the village only had a splattering of dirty snow left, mostly on the curbs and in the shadows of the big trees. When Devon showed up at the Cock & Bull the following day, he noticed a wet spot on the ceiling and a puddle on the floor. He got out a pan, and put it under the leak. Wasn't the first time this had happened, and he knew the roof needed repairs. He'd tried to get the leasing company who owned the strip of buildings along Main Street to spring for a new roof at the beginning of summer, but his calls had gone unanswered, his written requests ignored.

Kyle walked in. "Hey. What's up?" Then he saw the bucket. "Shit. Not again."

Devon nodded. He was sick and tired of fighting faceless people over a problem that shouldn't be his. He and his brother paid a friggin' fortune to lease the property, and the structure was not their responsibility to maintain. Since the existing owners, a mortgage company, hadn't done a damn thing to fix the roof during the dry season and the winter storms were already here, the problem now fell, like a lump of wet snow, on his shoulders.

"I'm hoping it can be patched up." He held his temper, not wanting Kyle to see how riled he was or how serious this situation could become. "We'll get a roofer out to have a look. Maybe then we'll get some action."

"Not damn likely," Kyle sniped. "They were sitting on their asses all summer and with the winter season here, it's too late."

"We'll figure it out." Devon kept his voice calm, knowing that one of them had to hold it together and keep a positive outlook. Being the eldest, he took on that job. Mila turned to him whenever she had a tough decision to make, and Kyle relied on him too. It was a lot of weight, but hell, what was a big brother to do?

Kyle glanced at the ceiling, watching the water drip. He was silent for some time, then said slowly, "Maybe it's time we unloaded the business. Should find something that isn't seasonal."

"Sell the bar? And do what?" Devon faced his brother. "What would you do with the money? Would you invest it? Use it for education? What big plans do you have?"

"I don't know. I'd stick it in the bank for now, get a job, figure things out."

"Yeah, and a couple of years from now, the money would be gone, and you'd be stuck as a bartender, or some dead-beat job, and never have a chance to be your own boss again."

"Hell, Dev. I don't want to sell the bar either. But I don't know how we can swing it. Every month there's another problem."

"It's too soon to give up. I really believe we can make a good livelihood here. And I'm not going anyplace. The mountains are my home, and if you're not committed to this, then you can walk away. I'll manage somehow."

Kyle got up and poured himself half a draft. "And how would you do that? It's tight enough as it is."

"Don't know, but I'll figure out something."

Visibly backing down, Kyle shoved a hand through his mop of curls. "I'm okay with whatever you decide. I've got no better place to go, and I like it here too."

They opened the bar that evening, but Devon couldn't shrug off his worry. What if they had to shut down for more than a few days? How much money would they lose? What if they couldn't pay the bank on time? Worries sure, but the one that gnawed on him was not so much about money as it was about Kyle. Would he be happier out of the bar?

At least he had one thing to be thankful for—Tara's falling asleep had been a blessing of sorts. The fact he hadn't had real sex with her would make it easier to bow out now before he got in any deeper. Had he done all the things he'd intended last night, blowing her off today would certainly seem callous.

* * *

Tara buried herself at work, attempting to block the memory of how Devon had walked away from her bed after barely sampling the goods. Obviously, he wasn't as in-to-her as she'd thought. Well, she refused to waste a minute worrying over the likes of him.

She had a new job to do, friends to make, and a full life ahead of her, with or without a man. Unfortunately, ever since she moved here, her libido had gone into overdrive. Perhaps it was the mountain air or that spring water Devon had talked about. She needed to get rid of it, that's for sure. She couldn't go around having all these erotic thoughts, especially when they all involved a man who could take her or leave her. Of course, it might be a whole lot worse if she was having them with every guy in town, which was certainly not the case.

Well, no more! She could be casual too. After all, she wasn't here to stay. It was just another small road on her path in life. No roots—that's what she wanted. No one to hold her down, or hold her back. He'd made it easy for her by leaving, and she should be grateful. He'd had more common sense than she did, and knew when to walk away. Next time she saw him, she'd be sure to thank him.

She finished her chores for the day, pleased with another good day's work. The hotel kitchen ran like a well-oiled machine with perfectly synchronized moving parts. From the executive chef to the lowliest dishwasher, the staff was experienced, efficient, and capable. They glided about, performing like ballet dancers, each one assisting the other by staying out of their way.

She freshened up, getting ready to leave, when Cindy waylaid her on the way out. "Hey, you up for a drink?"

"Sure. How about that dancing place you mentioned? I'm in the mood to cut loose."

"All right then!" Cindy tossed her head. "What's going on? I thought you had a thing for that bartender, Devon?"

"Hardly. He's not my type. If I had a type, which I don't, it would be someone with loftier goals. Kind of like me."

Cindy giggled. "They say opposites attract. If you met a workaholic, when would you have time for fun?"

"I'm sure we'd enjoy doing things together."

"Oh, please. Can you imagine falling for someone like Marc or Philippe?" She stuck her finger down her throat, pretending to gag. "Give me a hot bartender any day."

"You can have him. I'm not interested. I just want to dance and work off some steam. That's all."

"You need a good lay, that's what you need."

"I do not." At Cindy's expression, she laughed. "Okay. Maybe you're right."

Before the girls showed up at the club, they had unbuttoned their shirts as far as they dared and traded in their flats for the killer heels they left in their locker. Lips painted, hair teased, they strutted into the noisy, neon-lit, pulsing dance-club and pushed their way onto the floor. They danced for a few minutes then went in search of a drink and a small table.

Half way to the bar, someone grabbed Tara's arm and pulled her back to dance. The place was crazy and fun, filled with beautiful women and guys on the hunt. She bounced from one guy to the next and it was at least a half hour before she got her first drink.

Of course there was no place to sit and enjoy it, but she stood at the edge of the crowded floor and watched

Cindy. Two men surrounded her, and she grinded with them both. Tara shook her head, amused at Cindy's antics. The girl loved being a tease.

Whereas she was a boring old stick in the mud. While other kids had been doing God knows what in their teens, she'd been taking care of her mother and the household chores. She didn't know how to have fun.

Perhaps it was time she learned. She gulped her drink, put the glass on the nearest table and joined the frantic scene on the dance floor. She immersed herself in the music, really cutting loose. She wriggled her bottom and rubbed up against someone.

Glancing up, she recognized the guy. Damn. It was Kyle, Devon's brother.

"What are you doing here?" she asked. "Shouldn't you be helping at the bar?"

"Nope. It's my night off. We have a regular guy who does the afternoon shift and a few evenings a week." He came in close, and shouted over the noise, "You having a good time?"

"Sure am. This is great." She gave her head a toss, letting her hair fly around her shoulders. "Love the beat." Actually, she didn't recognize the music or understand the lyrics. The words garbled together, but the frenzied beat had everyone on their feet, including hers.

"Black-Eyed Peas."

"Southern dish. I've never tried that."

Kyle laughed. "It's the group. You must know Fergie?"

"The one who was married to the Prince?"

"No." He wiped his brow. "Wow. Do you get out much?"

"Guess not. I work too hard." Unlike that brother of yours, she wanted to add. She had ambitions whereas Devon was happy tending bar, skiing every day, and would never dream of leaving the mountains he so loved.

"Devon was in a piss-poor mood today. Every time he comes back from Serendipity Falls he gets a little strange."

"How's that?"

"Slammed the door when he came in last night. I heard him cursing up a storm too. When I got up this morning, he was already gone. Skiing at the crack of dawn. I don't know what his problem is, but I thought it might have something to do with you."

"With me?" She leaned in close and shouted, "Hardly. We're barely friends."

"Not the way I see it. He can't take his eyes off you when you come in."

"Really?" She stopped dancing. "I thought he didn't date local girls."

"You're not local, believe me." Kyle slowed his movements too. "Some of the girls up here, hell they are wilderness chicks. Not into that whole shaving their armpits thing."

Tara laughed and moved her feet again. "Well, I'm sure that won't be a problem with me. Legs either."

He glanced down, eyeing her pencil skirt and legs for the first time. "Good. You've got great legs. It would be a shame to hide them in fur."

"Thanks, buddy-boy." She glanced over his shoulder, and was frozen with a stare. "Hey, who's that girl giving me the evil eye?"

"My girlfriend, Lisa." He gave her a last twirl, then said, "Better go, before she cuts me off."

"Catch you around."

Tara went back to the bar, ordered a drink, and waited for Cindy to join her. When she did, she raised her voice over the music, and told her friend that she was ready to go. "Noise is giving me a headache. And I've danced for over an hour straight."

"Okay," Cindy said, glancing around. "But there's a lot of cute guys in here tonight. You're going to miss out."

"I guess I'm just not all that interested." Tara slid off the bar stool. "See you tomorrow. Have fun."

This time Tara willfully drove her car past the Cock & Bull, refusing to let it stop on its own accord. She needed to stay away from Devon, although her heart felt heavy and her stomach clenched at the thought.

CHAPTER SIXTEEN

It was hard not knowing what you wanted out of life. She had thought she did. After graduating from high school, she'd set her sights on culinary school and had done very well too. After completing the first year at the Lincoln Culinary Institute, she'd flown the coop, so to speak, going to New York to further her studies and earn a double diploma. After that she took jobs as far away from Orlando, her hometown, as she could find.

She'd been driven and eager to show her mark, moving upward in the chain of command. She'd relished moving about and enjoyed the challenge of living and working in a new environment. But that hadn't taught her a thing about herself. She had no idea how to have fun. To her fun was making a soufflé, or whipping up a fancy, out-of-this-world dessert. Respect and accolades from her peers was fun too.

All work and no play could make her a dull girl. She needed to work on that—being one dimensional was so limiting.

Sure, she'd had a boyfriend in Orlando. He'd been one of the instructors at the Lincoln Culinary Institute and he'd taught her a few things unrelated to cooking. She'd enjoyed those lessons too, but after six months he'd moved on to another young student. There'd been a guy in New York as well. He'd been a struggling actor, drop dead gorgeous, and very needy. It was all-me, me, me, with him. Then she'd dated someone in Vegas--he'd been exciting, a big spender with a big laugh, a big heart, and a big gambling habit. Beverly Hills had brought her Jared who looked like a model, wore snazzy expensive suits, drove around in his new Porsche, and was an account executive for a big advertising firm. The only thing he didn't advertise was that he had a wife and a baby on the way.

She'd thought she'd been in love with these men, but really, her pride had been wounded more than her heart. She loved to read thrilling romance stories, and yearned to feel that kind of deep, soaring passion. But not one man had ever come close.

From the time Tara left home, she knew the kind of men she wanted to date. Professional men who wore suits to work, who went to fine restaurants, enjoyed the symphony and theatre, and vacationed in Europe.

Devon would never fit that profile, which meant he wasn't a threat to her plans. Right? So what was she worried about? Silly girl, that meant he was safe. No way would she fall in love or want to marry a ski bum with no ambition. Would never happen. He'd be like all her other boyfriends. A mere diversion, not the main event.

She smiled, feeling happy again. She didn't need to worry about poor old Devon. Matter of fact, if he was willing, the two of them could have fun and sex, with the understanding that a time limit was in place. A year from now she'd be out of here, finding excitement in some new Cascade resort. Hawaii sounded good—not Maui since his parents lived there and he might come visiting, but one of the other islands.

With that thought firmly entrenched in her head, she happily removed her make-up, and undressed to go to bed. She snuggled under the duvet cover, and allowed her mind to drift. Devon was perfect for her needs. A man like him would know a lot about women, and hopefully be willing to teach her the things she didn't know.

Things like sex, doing it in more ways than one. She didn't want to be one-dimensional and ordinary in anything. If she were to be a sexual partner then she wanted to be an accomplished lover. Perhaps even sensational.

She would talk to him about it tomorrow. It all made perfectly good sense, and she was above all, a very sensible girl. They both could get something out of this mutual friendship or attraction, whatever they chose to call it. She was a quick learner and with his skills, surely, she'd become very efficient fast.

She smiled to herself, not imagining that he might disagree. After all, he'd been willing enough to get her into bed and even though she hadn't pleased him yet, she was more than willing to try.

The following day, Tara dressed carefully for work. She wore a form fitting black dress with a grey blazer, silky black hose, and sexy shoes to be worn once work was done. She dove into the day's affairs, barely coming up for breath. The eight hours flew by, and still kept on.

Once she was satisfied that the kitchen could survive without her, she left the hotel, eager to tell Devon about her new plan.

Instead of driving straight there, she went home to shower and change. The sexy dress and hose might work on the man she planned to marry, but skinny jeans would catch Devon's attention. And until she learned more practical skills about how to please a man, she wouldn't be ready to meet the one of her dreams.

Once she was suitably attired for the Cock & Bull, in a knit sweater and vest, tight jeans and boots up to her knees, she sauntered in and headed straight for the bar.

"Hey, there," she called to Devon.

He turned around slowly. "What's up, Tara?"

"Oh, not much. I just wondered if you and I could talk when you have a minute."

"Sure. But you can see," he indicated the number of people stacked up behind the bar seats waiting for drinks, "I'm a little busy now."

She smiled, but he didn't smile back. "Got that. When you have a minute, I'd love a Cosmo."

"Right after I serve all these other customers who've been patiently waiting."

"Oh." Her cheeks burned. "Oh. Of course. I'll just wait my turn."

"Why don't you do that?"

A dash of disappointment coiled inside her. He was certainly not chipper tonight. Kyle had been right. Something had crawled up his ass and she didn't think it was the infamous love bug either. This may not be the ideal time to bring up her ingenious idea of having him as her personal sex instructor, but heck, she was already here, so she might as well stay and enjoy herself.

She shrugged her shoulders and headed over to the pool table, where she took up a stance next to the wall and watched the young men play.

They noticed her too. "Can I buy you a drink?" one fellow asked. He looked to be in his forties, with a plaid shirt and a pot belly. Definitely not marriage material, but he had a cute face, and a nice smile.

"If you can get that stiff at the bar to give you one. He was too busy to serve me."

"That right, little girl? Well, I'm sure I can do better. What are you having?"

"I told him already. A Cosmo, but I'm more than happy to pay for it."

"Save your money. Let me see if I can rustle up that drink." She watched him walk away and noticed he had a nice butt too. When she glanced up, she locked eyes with Devon, and she knew he'd seen where she'd been looking.

Serves him right. Should have given her that drink.

He cocked an eyebrow and gave her a lazy, sexy smile as if he knew what she was thinking. Her blood temperature soared. Why the hell did he have to be so seriously hot? If he'd agree to be her sex teacher, she'd have to keep her heart in an iron-clad guard.

Cute butt guy was talking to Devon now, and he turned and winked, taking his wallet out of his back pocket. Devon handed him the Cosmo, but refused his money. They both had their eyes on her, and she felt uncomfortable, knowing she was playing them both, and not wanting to be that kind of girl. Hell, she wasn't that kind of girl.

She put her hands in her front pockets, shrugged, and gave an innocent smile to both men.

Hot buns returned and handed her the drink. "You know that guy? He wouldn't let me pay."

"Yeah, kind of. My car was in a ditch and he gave me a ride up the mountain."

"I see." His brown eyes looked like he could see a lot. "My name's Brad. Brad Henley."

"Nice to meet you, Brad." She shook his hand. "I'm Tara Reynolds, new pastry chef at the Cascade Grande."

"Well, I'll just have to come by some time and try out one of those pastries, won't I?"

"That would be a pleasure. I hope you do." She touched the rim of her glass with his beer. "Cheers."

"Cheers." He indicated the table. "You shoot pool?"

"Not well, but I do."

He nudged up to her. "When the guys are through I'll take you on, if you're up to it."

"I could manage a game or two." She stepped back, putting a little distance between them. Guy was crowding her space.

"What other games do you like to play?" he asked with a teasing grin.

"Backgammon, chess, to name a few." She glanced over at Devon, then turned her back so she wouldn't keep looking. "I ski a little, and play tennis too."

"Ah—board games and sports." His smile had a devilish look to it. "Nice, but I like things spicier."

"I'm not the spicy type," she mumbled, wishing she'd declined the drink after all. She was giving Brad the wrong idea, and she really needed to talk to Devon.

"I've never met a pastry chef before." He slipped an arm around her waist, and leaned down to whisper in her ear. "I bet you're sweet, aren't you?"

She pulled away, but he pulled her back. "Where are you going?"

She pushed at his chest. "You're getting a little too friendly, chum."

"That right?" Smiled again. "I have a better idea than shooting pool." His hand moved an inch lower on her back, edging toward her ass. "Why don't we get out of here soon?"

"That's not going to happen. Please take your hand off me."

"What's the problem? I'm only flirting. Isn't that what you're here for?"

"You heard the lady. Hands off." Devon had appeared out of nowhere, and stood right behind Brad.

Brad turned his head. "Glad you came over. We'll have another round."

Devon ignored him and asked Tara, "You okay with that? You want to drink with this guy?"

"No." She shook her head and glanced at Brad. "It was nice meeting you, but you're moving way too fast."

"You came on to me," he said with a smirk.

"I did not." Her eyes flew to Devon and he had a murderous expression on his face. "I didn't, Dev. I really didn't."

He gripped her arm and hissed, "It seems like we need to have that talk after all. Why don't you go home and I'll catch you later."

"Okay." She glanced at both men, feeling like a young girl being sent to her room. Dammit! She'd come here in an attempt to loosen up—and shed the skin of that emotionally stunted person she'd always been. Not to be manhandled by some over eager jerk, or told what to do by a guy that hooked up with only out-of-town women.

She pulled her arm away. "No. I'm going to meander around the bar and talk to anyone I choose."

Brad looked at Devon. "Is she always this annoying?"

He nodded in the affirmative. "You have no idea."

Tara flounced off and went in search of someone she might know. Not a single person. She realized she only had two choices. Go home or back to the bar and face Devon. Option two seemed more appealing, especially for a fun loving girl like herself.

The place had emptied out some, so she found a seat and waited for him to come over. "You want a drink?" he asked.

"Uh-yeah. I'm not sitting here just to look at you."

He grinned. "You wouldn't be the first girl."

"Really? You have a high opinion of yourself, don't you?"

"It's the truth. A month from now this place will be hopping and the city girls go after what they want. I get propositioned darn near every night." He shrugged. "Kyle too."

"No wonder you like city girls. You don't have to work for it."

"That's true." He handed her a freshly made Cosmo, and wiped the counter around her. "Since I work most nights, I don't have time to be chasing women, so saying yes once in a while makes good sense."

"I see." She twirled her seat around so she wouldn't have to look at him.

"So what did you want to talk about?" he asked. "I know you're sitting here for a reason."

"It's not important." She tasted her Cosmo but it was bitter on the tip of her tongue. She didn't want to drink…she wanted to… She didn't know what she wanted and that was the damn truth. How could she be happy if she didn't know what she desired?

"Out with it." He sighed. "Something's eating you. What is it?"

She turned back, and gave him a cold, hard look. "I was going to suggest trying, you-know-what, out again. But I don't think I'll make that offer." She tilted her nose in the air and pouted. "Not now, when you'll be so busy with your city girls."

"I could give it another shot. Things don't get real busy for another week or two," he said, topping it off with a sexy grin.

She felt her pulse shoot up, and hated the reactions she had around him. He got her motor running all right, and he damn well knew it.

"Since you'll be so busy, maybe I should find someone else to help me."

He stopped rubbing the counter top, and gave her a long look. "Help you with what? What do you want from me?"

"The same thing as the other girls. A good time. No commitment. I want to learn a lot of things that I think you'd like to teach me."

He leaned over, his face inches from hers. "Like what?"

"As you may have already noticed, I'm not that experienced. I want to enjoy sex more, without falling in love every time."

"Seems to me you enjoy sex quite nicely."

She glared at him. "What's that supposed to mean?"

"You know. You're quick to please."

"Could say the same thing about you." She glanced away. "And I'm not like that with other men."

"That case--what stopped you from hooking up with Brad? He seemed more than willing."

"You stopped me. I want to learn from you." She shifted closer to the bar, and spoke quietly, "Whatever I do, I like to do it well. And obviously, I'm not a star at this love making thing."

"I can teach you to ski like a pro, but I can't help you with that."

She pouted. "Why not? Was I that bad? Do you dislike me so much?"

"I don't dislike you at all. Quite the contrary. But you're a complication I don't need. This bar doesn't run by itself. My brother and I are up to our eyeballs in debt, and I'm just trying to squeeze out a living." He glanced at her. "Besides, like I've told you, I don't do relationships."

"That's perfect because neither do I." She flashed a bright smile. "Come by later, and we'll talk more."

"That's not a good idea. When the winter season gets busy I like to keep things casual."

"Me too. Think of me as one of your city girls, only more available." She slid off the bar. "See you later. We can work out the details."

He shook his head. "You're one of the strangest women I've ever met."

"And that's saying something, considering how many cross your path."

"I'll come by, but don't expect much."

"I never do." She winked. "I'll be waiting up."

At home, she ran around lighting candles, then tossed a log on the grate. Once the fire was going, she put on some nice music, not the ear-popping noise that she'd been dancing to at the club.

She took off her thigh high boots, changed from a sweater to a tank top, and sat down to wait.

CHAPTER SEVENTEEN

It was at least forty-five minutes until Devon showed up. She opened the door and threw her arms around him. He used his foot to kick the door shut, and thigh to thigh walked her toward the sofa. She fell backward and he landed on top.

They didn't break their kiss, and things got hot very quickly.

She had his belt buckle undone and he had her bra off, and his hands were full of her breasts. He bent his head to suckle her nipple and she whimpered with delight. Oh, he was a masterful teacher, and she was so eager to learn.

"Mmmm," she mumbled, her lips against his neck. "I like that. Can I touch you?" she asked, unzipping him and taking him in her hand. She stroked his shaft then allowed her fingers to rub over the tip of his penis, feeling a hint of moisture.

"Are you ready?" she asked. "I want to make sure you come first, don't forget."

"That isn't necessary," he answered, grinding her mouth with hot, wet kisses. His hands had left her breasts and one tugged at her jeans. The other was on her ass, pushing her gently into him.

"This is so hot," she whispered. "Can I help you with anything? Like remove my jeans?"

He jumped up. "Good idea." He grabbed her hand. "Right here in front of the fireplace or upstairs in bed?"

"Here. It's perfect."

She dropped her jeans to her ankles, and stood before him in a thin tank top and a lacy thong. She felt no shame. Only a deep, burning heat from inside of her, deep in her core and spreading through her belly, her loins. So intense were her feelings, she could almost cry.

Instead, she smiled, and he smiled back.

"You're beautiful," he said.

"So are you." She reached out a hand and drew him near. "Are you sorry I asked you here?"

He put a hand over hers, and encouraged her stroking. "What do you think?" He kissed her again tenderly. Then broke away long enough to remove his shirt and her tank. Her breasts were pressed into his big, brawny chest, and she continued to stroke him, as he did her.

Sliding a finger under the lace of her panties, he whispered, "You're wet."

"Is that a problem?" she answered, giving him hot, open-mouthed kisses.

"God, no." His tongue mingled with hers, and heat flared between them.

She gasped. "Devon. Don't stop. Please, don't stop."

"Are you ready?"

She nodded, unable to speak.

He grabbed a condom out of his jeans, slipped it on, then pulled her to him and entered her quickly. "Hold on, because this one's coming fast and furious."

She grabbed onto his shoulders, and leaned against the sofa as he drove her hard. He was panting and sweating, and she dug her nails into his butt, bringing him even closer than he had been before. "Now, do it now."

With a bellow, he found his quick release, then sank onto the rug, taking her with him. His arms wrapped around her, and he kissed her softly. Beside the fire, they laid in each other's arms. Slowly, she began moving next to him, and he licked her belly, her thighs, between her legs, and she withered beneath him, wondering why she'd never enjoyed this before.

He pleasured her for a long time, and she cried and begged him to stop, but he relentlessly pursued, tasting her, sucking gently on her sweet spot until she shuddered and came.

"This is unreal. I've only climaxed four times in my life, and two of them have been with you."

He raised himself to look at her. "What? Didn't the guys take care of you?"

"They were good lovers, just not great." She bit her bottom lip, feeling foolish. "I figured it was me. Some women have a hard time, you know."

"Not you. The men you slept with fell down on their job." He gave her shoulders sweet little kisses, while his hands toyed with her breasts. "You're a very passionate person."

She smiled. "You think so? So how did I make out?" If this was lesson one, she should be getting an A in love-making soon.

"What do you mean?" he mumbled, while his mouth grazed down her neck.

"I mean as an inexperienced lover, how did I do?"

He looked up. "What? You want a grade now?"

"Yes!" she said with a giggle. "I never knew sex could be so much fun."

"It is fun. Or should be."

"Dev, I don't expect you to be exclusive. I know that you want to be with other women. But whenever you're in the mood, I'd love more lessons from you." She kissed him sweetly. "Many, many more. Thanks for remembering the condom..." She scrunched up her nose. "I don't want to get a disease."

"You won't. I practice safe sex only." He leaned on an elbow and gazed into her eyes. "But is that all you want? You're not going to cry foul if I see another girl?"

"No. I promise." She ran light fingers up his back, making him shiver. "Thing is, I'm tired of being so rigid all the time." She kissed his shoulder. "I want to lighten up and stop being so serious."

"I'm pretty sure I can help you with that. Anything else?"

"No. I'm good." She grinned. "I'm not out to make a dramatic change. I like things as they are."

"And how's that?"

"Well, for one thing it's important for me to be successful. I want a better life than my parents. They never had any money, especially once Mom got sick and after she died,

Dad had lost so much money he had to sell the house."

"Besides the financial concern, it probably contained too many sad memories for him, as well. Moving might have been his best option." Devon wrapped a curl around his finger, playing with her hair. "Must have been really hard on you, losing your mother."

"Yes. We were very close, but seeing her so sick was even more heart-breaking. Watching a person go through chemo, and more than once, well, it was hideous. For all of us."

"I'm sorry," he said, and kissed her brow.

"Thanks. I still miss her and always will." She moved away slightly, so she could see him better. "It was the worst year of my life. We moved into an apartment my senior year of high school, and I remember how much fun all my friends were having and how excited they were about everything, but for me, it was like I was in a big black hole. Not nice. Anyway, I escaped the following year, when I started culinary school."

"You've always loved to cook?"

"After Mom got sick I had no choice, and then I discovered I had a knack for it. I love what I do. It brings me joy to put a smile on the faces of my happy customers, when they bite into one of my sinfully good delicacies. Chocolate could probably solve a lot of problems in the world."

He laughed. "You are terribly sweet. Know that?"

"I'm not sweet. I'm tough. And the point is—the career I chose opened my eyes to the world, and made me realize that I don't want to get stuck in one town again. I want to be free like a bird, and fly high."

"Fly where? What's so bad about this place? I can't imagine moving all the time."

"No, it's not ideal for most people. I understand you have your roots here and the mountain is your home." She shifted and gave him a kiss. "I don't want to be transferred anytime soon, but normally I get restless after a year or so."

"I could probably take a year of you." He smiled and kissed her fingers.

"I intend to move forward in my career path and I don't want to get sidetracked. But after meeting you all I can think about is sex. It's a little crazy, don't you think?"

"Not crazy, but addictive. You have the same effect on me. Every time you're near, I'm blind-sided."

"It's not like anything I've ever experienced before. But I like it."

"Which part?"

She felt her cheeks warm, and turned her head. "You know, all of it. Making love. Making out."

"Come on, baby." He gave her a lazy smile. "Say the word. I want to hear it from that pretty mouth of yours."

"What word?" She gazed into his eyes, feeling the heat rise between them.

"Fuck. You want to fuck me."

"Yes." She breathed deeply and closed her eyes, then rolled on top of him. Her fingers stroked his cheek, then lightly caressed his lips. "I do. Again and again."

"Again."

She kissed him slowly, and felt him stir beneath her. "Are you up for it?"

"I'm getting there. Just stay where you are." He grabbed another condom and slipped it on.

"Who's going to come first?" she asked with a playful smile.

"Doesn't matter. But it's your turn."

She positioned herself over him and took him in deep, rocking gently against him. "Is this okay?"

He gritted his teeth. "It's fine. Better than fine, but do we have to talk about it?"

"No. I'm just checking." She arched her back and he took hold of her breasts, and played with her nipples. "I like that."

"You're still talking," he mumbled, nipping on her shoulder.

She smiled and bent over to kiss him. "Fuck me, Dev. Fuck me like you mean it."

Heat and passion soared between them, lifting them higher, and higher still, until they reached the peak and toppled over, both at the same time.   "Oh, my. Oh, my. Was that like...it was, right? I mean I've read about it in books but never experienced it myself. You did come, right? I mean, we both did."

"Tara, could you please be quiet for a moment? I'd like to enjoy the aftermath of that explosion," he gasped.

"That's fine. Go right ahead. I'm going to take a shower. Lay here as long as you want."

She rolled over, then ran off to take a shower. She had lathered herself and was ready to rinse when she heard him enter. She turned to him with a welcoming smile.

He took the soap from her hands and began to wash her back, her legs, between her thighs. She was tender down there, but it was a good ache. "I'm a little sore," she said, and removed his hand.

"I'm sorry." He guided her under the shower head so she could rinse.

"No one has ever washed me before," she told him, blinking water out of her eyes.

"Another first." He kissed her neck. "Did you like it?"

"Mmm. Very nice." Her eyes rested on his mouth. "You're very nice. I give you an A plus in every subject."

"Hey, I thought I was the teacher."

"Problem is--I'm a quick learner."

She moved out of his reach, and stepped out of the stall, wrapping a towel around herself. "It just occurred to me that the second part of this equation might get difficult."

"What part is that?"

"Not letting my emotions get involved."

"Tara." His eyes slid away from hers. "You know how I feel about that."

"I know and I couldn't agree more." She held the towel like it was a life preserver. She looked down at the floor, not willing to share with him how much her heart ached just looking at him. He'd be scared off if he knew she had feelings—that wasn't a part of their deal.

"No, buts," he said. "I'm going to be pestered by city girls and you're going to set the local boys on fire. Right?"

"I guess so." She looked at him. "But I'm not going to like those city girls doing all the things I want to do with you."

He stepped out of the shower, dripping wet, gloriously naked. "We agreed to this. Do you want to call it off?"

"No." She stared at him, heart pumping. "Do you?"

"Not a chance. I like you, Tara. Just being with you."

"That's good for now. But I think you're fooling yourself. A guy like you needs to be married, with a bunch of children hanging around. You'd make a great dad."

"Maybe one day. I can barely afford myself right now. Until I'm financially stable, the last thing I want is a family hanging around my neck."

She made a face. "You make that sound so romantic."

"We aren't supposed to be about romance. Besides, I didn't mean it like that. I just don't need the extra worry."

"Fair enough. I'm not in the market anyway." She went into the bedroom and slipped on a robe.

The bathroom door was still open and she watched him dry off. Her throat constricted and she felt a sharp pain. Keeping her emotional distance would be a problem. But she had always welcomed the joy of falling in love. What would it take for it to stay?

CUPID

Rubbing my hands together, I couldn't help but giggle and give a smug smile. Things were certainly looking up. That love making scene had gone particularly well if my ears hadn't misinformed me. They both had sounded extraordinarily happy and they couldn't stop smiling and touching each other. I knew I hadn't been wrong putting these two handsome creatures together. Both had seemed very lonely when I first laid eyes on them at the Falls restaurant, and look at them now. They can't take their eyes off each other, and even though they still protest too much, it's obvious that neither of them would want to go back to the way they were before.

People need love to be happy, and after a hundred and eighty years on earth no one can tell me different. I know what I'm doing. And it's probably safe for me to leave and find someone else who's unhappy, but I might just stick around a little longer and make sure they don't screw things up.

Funny how humans have a way of doing that. They are so protective of their hearts and make so many excuses why they can't love each other and be together, when in reality all they have to do is accept their fate and embrace it.

CHAPTER EIGHTEEN

Devon left the house around midnight, but tearing himself away from Tara hadn't been easy. She got under his skin, and it had little to do with the sensational sex. She was smart, confident, sexy, and likeable. Too darn likeable, and that was half the problem.

He'd built a good reputation around town, and he didn't want to blow it over one girl. He had no one to blame but himself, since he was the one who'd guzzled that damn spring Serendipity water. He hadn't wanted to admit it to Tara, but yes, he'd had a bottle the day he met her. And everything had been topsy-turvy since.

The one thing he'd learned in all his years as a practicing stud was that sex and friendship didn't work. You couldn't have both, and he didn't want to lose her as a friend.

Like Kyle said, he was toast. Might as well start planning his own damn wedding.

Unless…unless there was some kind of antidote.

The following morning he drove down to Serendipity Falls. He didn't have a plan in motion, but decided to try out a health food shop first. At least he wouldn't feel like a complete idiot in a place that sold alfalfa, and wild blue-green algae to their customers.

Few years back he'd dated a girl who was a health nut and would drink wheat grass juice every morning for breakfast, and lived on minerals that contained chlorophyll. After a couple of months they parted ways, unable to agree on most everything. He went back to eating red meat, red wine, and waffles for breakfast and had managed to live happily ever after.

The health food store was in the mall, so he figured he'd better stop in and see Mila while he was there. He bought a couple of lattes from Starbucks, figuring she might like one.

"Dev. What are you doing back in town?" She smiled and gave him a big hug, then scooped one of the lattes out of his hands. "This for me? Thanks. Looks yummy."

He kissed her cheek. "Yeah, I had to come in for a couple of things. Figured I'd stop by and see how you're making out."

"Oh, you know. I'm so busy, I can hardly see straight. Another wedding this weekend, and I've got to get the invitations out, find a florist, order a cake. Just the usual stuff."

"Sounds to me like you're more of a wedding planner than an owner of a boutique. Do you charge for this work?"

"Not exactly, although I make a percentage. You see, my customers are always in such a rush and don't want to wait to organize a proper wedding, so I help out where I can. I'm compensated plenty, because they buy almost everything from me, and I take a small commission from the florists and the bakery shop, etc."

"You're a genius, my dear sister." He took a drink of his coffee, and eyed her for a moment. "What about you? Why don't you find Mr. Right?"

"Heck. I'm not ready yet. But you?" She laughed wickedly. "Now you're another story. So where's Tara? Is she here with you? She's perfect, by the way."

"She's all right. But no, I came alone. And we are not getting married, so get that little thought right out of your head." He rubbed his jaw. "We're barely dating. More like sex pals."

"You're disgusting, you know that?" She punched his arm. "Anyway, I know couples in love when I see them. Should, since they come in here every day. And you two? You've got it, I'm happy to say."

"Like hell we do." He had a terrible feeling begin in his gut.

"I'll put a wager on it." She crossed her arms and gave him a cocky look. "I'm an astute business woman. How much do you want to lose?"

He laughed, defensive and determined to beat this case of, whatever it was. "Don't waste your money." He glanced toward the store windows. "Looks like you might have another pair of suckers coming in."

She glanced over his shoulder. "Oh, goodie. I love all this excitement. It's the best job ever. And I can't wait to help you and Tara plan your upcoming nuptials."

"That will be a frosty Friday."

"Funny you said that. We're expecting frost this weekend." Mila grinned and shooed him out. "Go away and don't scare off my customers. And thanks for the latte."

Devon held the door open for the two lovebirds who probably didn't know what hit them, and never would. They'd be committed to a marriage without end. Poor lovesick fools.

He wandered down the shopping center until he found the health food store. He walked in and spotted a young girl alone at the front counter. She had orange hair, tats on her arms, and piercings on her bottom lip. She had to help him. He was determined not to be led to the slaughter like that couple he'd just seen.

"Hi." He gave her a friendly smile. "Can you tell me if you sell anything to counter the after effects of the local spring water?"

"Uh- like what?" The girl answered. "Spring water is good for you. I drink at least a gallon a day."

"Doesn't it make you feel weird?" He gave her a quick once over. "Have you had any improper thoughts or inclinations after drinking it?"

"Excuse me?" Her eyes narrowed, and she took a protective step back. "Are you some kind of whack job? Do I need to call the police?"

"No, I was just wondering if other people who live around here have come in and complained about the water making them have strange thoughts?"

She moved to the cash machine at the end of the counter. "I have a panic button, right here. If you don't leave I'm going to press it."

"I'm not dangerous. I just need an antidote for the spring water. Have you heard of one? Know where I can get it?"

"One second," she warned, "and I'm pressing the button."

He took two steps backward. "It's the love bug," he blurted. "I think I caught it, and can't get rid of it."

Her eyes grew big. "Oh!" She clapped her hand over her mouth. "I haven't met anyone who's had it before. How cool."

"It's not cool," he answered stiffly. "And I need to get rid of it before it destroys my life."

"But that's what's so wonderful about this place." Her voice rose with excitement. "Everyone falls in love, they marry, and it's like, forever. Divorces are unheard of around here. You are so lucky. You will live and die a very happy man."

"Over my dead body." He gave her a horrified look then practically ran out of the store. Head down, he walked out of the mall, muttering under his breath. "There has to be something to get rid of it. I'm not getting married, that's for damn sure."

"Watch it, dude," a guy said after he Devon bumped into him.

"Fucking love bug," he snapped as people skirted around him. He knew he was frightening some of the mall shoppers, but didn't give a damn.

He was ready to hightail it back to Mammoth but decided to stop for a quick bite at the Falls café. The scene of the crime. He had a thing or two to say to that frizzy haired waitress. After all, she had served Tara the water, and should know a hellova lot better.

Sue Burke came over to him. "Hey, how's it going? How's our mutual friend, Tara? You two still an item?"

"We are not an item. Never have been and never will be." He studied the table, and felt heat flood his face. "That's why I'm here. I wondered if you know anyone who's ever drank the water and been infected by a virus."

Confused for a moment, her face cleared and her eyes shone bright. "You mean the love bug? That's it—right?"

He nodded. "I need to get it out of my system."

"No, you don't!" She beamed. "Why, you are one lucky dog."

"I can't have this." He sank onto a stool. "There has to be a way to get rid of it."

"Don't think so." She put a hand on her hip, and looked out the window with a dreamy expression on her pleasant face. "It's supposed to be wonderful. Cherish it. You just don't understand how lucky you are."

"I don't want to cherish it. I want an antidote. I can't afford a wife. Has anyone ever escaped it?"

Sue smiled with very little sympathy. "Til death do you part, I'm afraid."

He cursed, and then felt something sting the back of his neck. He turned around but couldn't see anything. He ordered a burger and a soda, and while he waited, he kept glancing around the other booths. Someone, somewhere had a high pitched giggle.

CHAPTER NINETEEN

Kyle was at the bar when Devon walked in. "Why are you looking so glum? I haven't even told you the good and the bad news yet."

Devon slumped down on one of the bar stools. "What's the good news?"

"The inspectors were here, and said the roof can be patched up and make it through the winter season. Said it's a temporary fix, which will end up more expensive in the long run."

"Hell, if the lease company won't respond to my calls, maybe we should stop paying the rent. See if that gets their attention."

"Yeah, like that's a great plan," Kyle muttered.

"Look. I'm plain out of ideas. Why don't you take over the problem for a change?" Devon closed his eyes and ran a hand over his face. "Maybe we'll have to sell out after all. That should make you happy."

"What the hell does that mean?" Kyle slammed a fist against the bar top. "Your attitude's never been great, but lately? Downright shitty. We need to sleep on it, and come up with a plan."

"Maybe someone rich and famous will walk in and want to be our sugar-momma," Devon muttered. "We need something good, that's for sure."

Kyle grinned. "That'd be nice. Heads I get her, tails you lose."

"Keep dreaming." Devon got off the stool and went behind the bar. "Let's hope for a lot of snow and that our business will pick up. Meanwhile, I'll work on my attitude."

They had a busy night but no famous person came in to take away their financial worries. The following day Devon got up early and took to the slopes. As usual, hard, fast skiing acted as a tonic for his troubled mind.

He took the gondola to the Summit, and hiked up another two hundred yards, alone with the world, in a place he liked to be. It was peaceful and quiet, the snow untouched and pristine. Tree branches were heavily laden, and frozen icicles sparkled as the sun peaked through. Wispy layers of clouds drifted in the bright blue sky.

Devon took several minutes to suck it all in, then he gripped his poles, and pushed off head first as the gravity allowed. His turns were quick and tight as he flew down the mountain slope, carving his way through the trees, the moguls, becoming air-borne for several heart-pounding moments. The energy flowed through him as it always did, and he felt exhilarated, his worries put on hold.

He was in a much better frame of mind when he showed up for work. He loved his life, and he wouldn't give up this existence for anything. Things would work out. They always did.

"Hey, Kyle. I might pop out for an hour. Go track down these invisible people who seem to get a kick out of ignoring me. They got to exist, right?"

"If you say so." He shrugged. "Go ahead, but I'm still hoping for that miracle."

Just then the door opened, and a tall, svelte, designer clad knock-out waltzed in.

Devon whistled under his breath. "Wow. Miracles do happen."

The two men turned to her with matching smiles. "We're not quite open," Devon said, "but for you we'll make an exception."

"I'm sorry, I know it's early, but I have to waste an hour because my room's not ready. I'm staying at the Cascade Resort. I could have lunched there but I wanted to see the town." She sat down at the bar, and took off her fur jacket, dropping it on the stool next to her. "It's a darling village."

Underneath the jacket, the lady wore an ivory turtle-neck cashmere sweater, which displayed her voluptuous bosom.

Kyle couldn't quite take his eyes off them and his mouth opened and closed like a guppy's. Finally he found his tongue. "Glad you came here. Aren't we, Dev?" He flushed, and smiled. "I'm Kyle, and this is my brother, Devon. And you found the best bar in town."

"Marissa Evans." She shook both their hands. "Nice to meet you," she purred.

"Welcome to Mammoth," Devon said. "You staying long?"

"Three-four days, but I'm sure I'll be back before the season's over."

"What can we get you?" Kyle asked. "Mojito, margarita, martini? The first drink's on the house."

"I'll have a chardonnay, but I insist on paying. Do you have Simi?"

"I think we do. Let me check." Devon found a bottle, opened it, and rushed to pour the lady's glass. "So where are you from?"

"Milan. But I'm here in L.A. for a couple of months. I do fashion design."

Kyle stammered, "I thought you looked like a model."

She laughed. "No, I don't model, but they wear my clothes." She gave him a flirtatious look. "My modeling days ended years ago. Now, I'm too old and too fat."

"Hardly. You don't look like you're thirty."

"That's ancient is this business. I stopped when I was twenty-five, and discovered that I like designing clothes and having other women wear them."

"Hell, I'd wear your clothes." Kyle said, his confidence returning.

She laughed again. "You are a very funny boy. Can you men join me in a drink, or is that not allowed?"

"We own the place, so we can make our own rules." Kyle poured another glass of chardonnay and sat down beside her. "So Milan is your home?"

"No. I'm actually from Russia, but now I work mostly in Milan."

"What brings you to L.A?" Devon inquired.

She ran a finger along the stem of her glass. Tilted her head back and smiled. "Rodeo Drive, baby. We have a big fashion show coming up. I'll be here for a few months." She took a sip of wine. "I love to ski, and before I get crazed, I figured I owed myself some relaxation time. Once I start work, I won't be able to come up for breath." Her big brown eyes darted from one man to the other. "Do either of you ski?"

The brothers looked at each other and laughed. "Do bears shit in the woods?" Kyle added, "Dev was an Olympic skier, and I learned when I was three."

"Wow, an Olympian. Congratulations." She gave Devon a dazzling smile. "I'm impressed. I'm not bad if either of you would like to ski with me, and have a few hours free."

"Holy crap," Kyle muttered. "I can't believe I'm going to have to say no. My girlfriend is a ski instructor and if she saw me with you, she'd chuck a fit. I can hook you up with her if you'd like an instructor."

"No, thanks. How about you, Dev?"

He thought about Tara and remembered his resolve not to get emotionally involved. This was just the diversion he needed. The perfect antidote to any existing love bug.

"Sure. I'm up for it. I'll pick you up at the hotel tomorrow, around eight am. I have to work in the afternoon, but that'll give us several hours."

She finished her wine. "Sounds great. I'll be in the lobby." She slid off the bar, then bent over to pick up a glove that had fallen to the floor. Both men had an excellent view of a perfectly rounded rump before she straightened up. "I'm glad I met you two." She took a twenty out of her purse. "Thanks for the drink, and I'll see you bright and early."

Devon tried to push the money back, but she wouldn't let him. "It's not every day I get to ski with an Olympian. I'm certainly not going to let you buy my drinks."

He put the bill in the till. "Enjoy the hotel. I hear the pastry is out of this world."

She patted her hips. "No, thank you. I don't need any extra padding."

Dev gave her the once over. "You can afford an ounce or two and the new pastry chef is a friend of mine." He could have bitten off his tongue. Why in the world had he gone and said that?

"Is that so? Seems like you two men have a lot going on in this town."

Dev felt heat creep up his neck. "Two bachelors. You know how it is."

"I do, and I've never minded a little competition either." She winked. "I'm looking forward to a challenge tomorrow."

CHAPTER TWENTY

The following morning Devon arrived at the Cascade Grande exactly on the hour, and not seeing Marissa, he took a seat in the lobby to wait. Snow was lightly falling, and the temperature was mild. He expected it to be a beautiful day.

He was staring out the window, when he heard her call out his name. She grinned and waved, and Devon felt like all eyes were on him as he got up from the chair and walked toward this stunning creature. She was all decked out like a Hollywood star, in a glitzy silver one piece suit that fitted her luscious frame as if it had been painted on. Her long dark hair was pulled off her face by a shiny silver headband, revealing her classic features, the big dark brown eyes, the perfectly straight nose, arched brows and lush, full lips. She was gorgeous and everyone in the room knew it.

When he reached her side, she put an arm through his and kissed his cheek, seemingly unaware that she was the center of attention. But then, he figured, she would be used to it. She'd been a model after all.

Beautiful, spoiled, rich, and more than a handful, he didn't doubt.

Underneath that sexy, ultra-cool exterior, he figured there would also be plenty of passion and fire. Just what he needed to get Tara out of his head. If this woman couldn't do it, he was a goner for sure.

"Come on, Dev. Take me skiing. I've been dreaming about this all night."

A doorman held the door open, and a bell-hop stumbled over a bag when he caught sight of her.

Devon hadn't moved. He was too busy watching the impact she had on people, and wondering why he wasn't feeling it. God, Tara got him worked up with just one glance, and yet this gorgeous spit-fire had zero effect. Well, he'd damn well see about that. No way was he going to succumb to some damn love bug. He'd fight it tooth and nail, and mind over matter.

She grabbed hold of his hand, gave it a tug, and then glided out the door.

They reached the top of the Sierra well before nine, and he took Marissa down a few black runs to get a feel for the way she handled the skis. After skiing the Climax, the China Bowl, and the Sanctuary, he knew she had not exaggerated her skills the day before—she was an expert skier who showed guts and a reckless determination not to be outdone. She flew over moguls, raced down the narrow slopes, pushing herself to keep abreast of him.

Devon was the one who couldn't keep up. He stopped at a viewpoint and sucked in some air. "Whoa, lady. This isn't a competition. Let's take a moment and enjoy the day."

"I am enjoying it," she told him. "It's exciting, don't you think?"

Her bright eyes glittered, reminding him of the exuberance he had once felt tearing up the slopes. Not so much anymore. The competitive drive was gone from his soul. Now, he only pushed himself when he felt the urge.

"Exciting, yes." He looked away from her. "I had a bad injury that ended my Olympic dreams. My legs can't take the abuse anymore. I'm sorry."

"Oh, I apologize." Her gloved hand reached out and touched his arm. "I didn't know."

"That's all right. How could you?" He smiled. "We can still ski our hearts out, but I'd rather not race. Go as fast as you like, and I'll follow at a more leisurely pace."

"Does it hurt?" she asked softly.

"No. It hurt when it ended my career, but the legs don't bother me much. I'm lucky enough that I can still get up here day after day."

"That is good," she agreed. "So, why don't you lead the pace and I'll be happy to follow." She flashed him a smile. "If I feel the need for speed, I'll meet you at the bottom of the lift."

"Fair enough." They skied for a couple of hours, then Devon said it was time for him to head back.

"I'm going to stay up and ski some more," Marissa announced. "Thanks for a wonderful day. It's a big mountain. Could have gotten lost."

"You would have been fine," he answered. "Guys would have fallen over themselves to help."

"But you knew all the best runs." She grinned. "Thanks again. If I'm not too bushed, I might drop by the bar tonight."

"Do that. I'd like to see you."

"Would you?" Her eyes carried a deeper meaning as they met his.

"Of course." He pushed thoughts of Tara out of his head. What did he have to feel guilty about? Absolutely nothing. Besides, she'd given him her blessing to see other girls. And he would give her the same option. Not that he expected she'd want to bed someone else. But the choice would be hers.

"You think I'm an idiot?" The sooner he got this luscious creature in bed, the sooner he could get rid of the spell Tara wove around his heart.

"No, I didn't say that. Just wondered about your pastry chef, that's all."

"I'm not exclusive with anyone, if that's what you want to know."

"It is. See you later," she said, then pushed off, heading for the nearest chair.

He took his time, picking his way to the bottom. There was less snow on the lower runs and some dry areas that needed to be avoided, but he never took the gondola down unless he had too. Some things were a matter of pride.

* * *

Tara was seething, having heard from Cindy about the gorgeous movie-star that Devon had met in the hotel lobby this morning. She was so angry she drove straight to the bar after work.

She stood in the doorway, her eyes snared by the sight of the drop-fucking-dead-gorgeous feline perched on the bar seat, leaning forward as if licking up the sight of Devon pouring drinks.

Tara's nails bit into the palms of her hands. She had no claim on Devon, but somewhere deep inside she felt he was hers. They had something together—or at least she thought they did. She may have told Devon she didn't mind him dating city chicks, but she had lied—to herself as much as to him.

She straightened her shoulders, lifted her chin and walked over, taking a seat at the other end of the bar.

He was so busy chatting with Miss Universe that he didn't notice her for a few long minutes. Finally, maybe he felt her gaze on him and glanced her way. Color rose from his open necked shirt and flooded his face. Caught in the act. Like a boy with his hand in the cookie jar, guilt written all over him.

If he felt guilty, he must have done something he shouldn't have. Her eyes narrowed, and she thought about walking out, afraid that she'd say something which would embarrass them both. But her rigid body wouldn't move. Like a frozen layer of strawberry ice, she sat there, fighting for control.

He strolled over. "Hey, Tara. I didn't expect to see you tonight."

"Obviously," she snapped. "I can see that you're busy."

He glanced around at the crowded room. "Yeah, we've got a good turn-out tonight."

"That wasn't what I meant." She tilted her head. "Who's the beautiful girl? Heard you went skiing together."

"How did you hear that?" He started mopping up the counter, not looking at her.

"Oh, you know what small towns are like. Everybody knows everyone else's business." She licked her lips. "So, who is she?"

"She's from Milan, but in L.A. for a fashion show. She's a designer."

"I see. Wow." She bit the inside of her cheek, trying hard to keep the hurt from showing, but it felt like a dagger to her heart. He'd not waited very long to get someone new in his bed. "Will she be staying long?"

"A few months. In Los Angeles, not here." He poured her a glass of chardonnay, and put it in front of her. "She's staying at your hotel for a couple of nights."

"That's nice. I hope she eats there too. I'll make something special just for her."

He grinned. "I doubt if she eats sweets."

Her nails dug into her hands like claws. "Neither do I. Seems like we have two things in common."

"Meaning?" He quirked a brow.

She ground her teeth. She didn't want to have this conversation, but she needed to know. "Meaning—did you sleep with her?"

"No, not yet." His eyes were steady on hers. "Which is not really open for discussion. We both agreed."

Tara picked up the glass of wine, and came *this* close to tossing it into his handsome face. "I see. So that's where we are. Or, should I say, where we were. You sleep with anyone you like, and I can do the same thing too."

"Right." He glanced at Marissa, who'd been watching them. "She's only here for a few days. If you find someone you'd like to sleep with, feel free."

"Right," she echoed back, then took a big sip of the wine. "I'm sorry if I got our signals crossed. You made it very clear that we weren't exclusive, and I understood that. Just didn't see it happening so soon. My mistake."

She slugged the rest of the wine down. "Have fun. She's very pretty." Tara slipped off the stool. "I'm not paying for the drink."

"I didn't ask you to."

She was heading out the door, when some young guy whistled to get her attention. The night air slapped her in the face, just as the guy reached her side.

"You're not leaving, are you? The night's young. Besides, it's cold."

She didn't want to talk to anyone. She wanted to go home and feel really crappy by herself. But the thought that Devon might be watching made her turn around with a smile.

"I might stick around a bit." She flipped back her hair and tossed him a flirty look. "So, do you play pool?"

"Sure. If you're up for it." He stuck out his hand. "Name's Jamie. Are you from around here?"

"Tara Reynolds. I moved here a few weeks ago. I work at the Cascade Hotel."

"Yeah? I work at one of the ski shops in town, but snowboarding's my thing."

"How's that?" She folded her arms under her breasts, and tilted her head to look at him.

"I compete in a lot of the aerial stuff."

"You're pro?" This news delighted her, if for no reason other than it might piss Devon off.

"Turned pro last year. You ever watch a competition?"

"Just on TV. It's pretty scary stuff."

He laughed. "It's the best. I'm working on a triple half pipe flip and I've pretty much nailed it."

"Wow. I'm impressed." She glanced at his beer. "I'm going to the bar for a drink. Can I get you another beer?"

"Sure." He lifted his bottle so she could see what he was drinking. "Thanks."

"You're welcome." She swayed her hips as she returned to the bar.

Devon was waiting for her. "He's not your type. The kid's only twenty-two."

"Is that right? I bet he's got a lot of stamina." She gave him a sexy smile. "He's going to need it."

"Don't go there. You don't want to mess with the locals. He's not going anyplace, and it'll get ugly. Trust me. I learned the hard way."

"I bet you did. But I like making my own mistakes." She turned to smile at Jamie. "He's having a beer and I'll have another wine. And you can skip the advice."

"You got it." He poured the drinks and slid them on the counter. "That'll be fourteen bucks."

"Better be good wine for that price."

"It is. Marissa only drinks the best. It's a Russian River. Unless you prefer the house swill."

She handed him a ten and a five. "Keep the change."

She took the two drinks and headed back to Jamie. "Here you go." She toasted him with her glass. "So when are you practicing next? I'd like to see a few of your stunts."

"I'm on the mountain every morning. If you're not working, come on by."

"I'll do that." She sipped from her glass. "Tell me about yourself, Jamie."

"Not much to tell. I started skateboarding when I was five, and just had a knack for it. In high school I entered some local competitions and began winning. By the time I was sixteen I'd picked up a few medals in professional competitions. I skipped college and just went for it. Now it's my life."

"How many events would you compete in during a year?" She shrugged. "I know so little about it."

"There's so many that I can't make because I'm not winning big enough. But I do a lot of the smaller competitions, and for the past three years I've been at the Winter X Games and the US Open. Haven't medaled in either of those, but I will soon. I feel it."

"That's awesome." She sipped her wine, smiling at him. "I'm so glad I ran into you tonight. I hope I'm not monopolizing your time."

"Not at all." He glanced around, and noticed her near empty drink. "You want to get out of here? You can come back to my place, and see my trophy room. If you're interested in snow-boarding I've got some greats videos we could watch. Or just make-out. That's up to you."

She laughed at his direct approach. "I have my own car. Why don't I follow you back, but I can't promise that I'll stay." He grabbed his jacket, and she went in search of her coat. She noticed Devon talking to his new friend, and struggled to keep her hurt inside. There was a deep ache, a vast hole where her heart used to be.

Well, it just might be time to start looking for a new place to work. Usually, when she felt like this she'd simply pack up and leave. She'd signed a one year contract, but that wouldn't be a problem. It never was.

This was her fault, of course. Why did she let men into her life, when she didn't want a commitment and they didn't either? Hadn't she learned a thing over the years? People left. They either died, or they just went away. The only person you could truly rely on was yourself.

She met Jamie at the door. "I'm ready. Lead on."

He held the door for her, and she glanced back. Devon had stopped talking to his fashion goddess and was staring at her and Jamie. She battled the urge to stick her middle finger in the air. Instead she slipped her hand in Jamie's pocket, and snuggled up to him as they left.

When they got to the parking lot she disengaged her hand, and stopped the pretense. She didn't want to go to bed with Jamie. She knew what she was looking for, and neither Jamie, nor Devon fit the image she'd carried around so long in her head.

"Jamie, I think I might head home after all. It's been a long day at work." She pecked his cheek. "I'm not ready to come back to your place, but I'll take a rain-check, if you don't mind?"

"Your loss," he said with a grin. "One day, you'll look back at this night and think to yourself—'self, I could have jumped that poor boy's bones, and now I have to stand out here in this freezing line just to get an autograph'."

"Yes, I can see that happening," Tara answered with a smile.

"And you won't get to see some of my really great moves."

"Maybe another time." She moved forward and kissed his lips. "It's nice to meet a man with passion, someone who is following his dreams. I hope yours all come true."

CHAPTER TWENTY-ONE

Devon watched her leave, knowing he should have done something to stop her. He didn't want her sleeping with Jamie, even though he liked and respected the kid very much. He didn't want her sleeping with anyone. Well, except himself.

But he'd thrown down the gauntlet, and she'd picked it up before he had a chance to think it through. He definitely didn't want any other guy giving her a sex education, that's for damn sure. He liked her. And if it meant giving up a night with Miss High Fashion, then so be it. Hopefully, when Tara found out he'd remained loyal and true she'd be appreciative of his sacrifice and not take a strip out of his hide.

Then again, maybe not. She had a sharp tongue, and a rigid viewpoint about certain things. And he had a pretty good idea that he'd ticked her off plenty. But she'd bounced right back, hadn't she? A little too well, he was afraid.

The bar was emptying out, and he felt okay about leaving it in Kyle's capable hands. If there were any problems at all, he had his cell and was only a quick call away.

"I'm heading out," he told his brother. "Got a couple of things I need to do."

"Yeah? Could Tara be one?"

"Not likely. I pissed her off, and she left with Jamie."

"Oops. You better get over there fast. You know he's got away with the girls."

"Shut up. You don't have to remind me."

"What about Marissa? Isn't she hanging around, expecting maybe a little something from you?"

"It can't be helped. If she asks where I've gone, cover for me. Make something up." He ran a hand through his hair. "Shit. This is bad. She's a nice lady, but I can't do this now."

"Man, you're crazy, dude. She's smokin' hot."

"She is, but it's not likely that I'd ever see her again, and I'd have blown my chances right here. Tara's worth it."

Kyle eyed him. "I've never heard you say that about a girl."

"Well, maybe I finally met one that I care enough about, or I'm just getting too lazy for the chase."

"Spring water, I told you. That's what it is."

"Cut the bullshit, would ya? You know I hate it when you talk like that."

"Sure. That's why I do it." Kyle grinned, and left him to go back to his customers.

Devon glanced at Marissa, and before he had a chance to change his mind, he headed straight out the door. Didn't even grab his jacket on the way out. He shivered as he walked to the car. A hot night with Marissa might have cured him of whatever the hell he was feeling for Tara, but maybe, just maybe, he didn't want to be cured.

He blew on his hands, and got the key in the lock. When his motor was running, he gave it a minute until the windows defogged and heat kicked in, then stepped on the gas. He knew where Jamie lived and if he saw her car there, he might just have to break down that door and do the whole caveman routine.

She was his, dammit. At least for now. She'd explained how important her career was to her and that soon she'd be moving on. He knew she had a one year contract, and the idea occurred to him that he could offer her the same. A less formal, but still binding contract to be faithful for the year, and when the time was up they'd part friends. Very civilized and economical.

More partnerships would benefit from this forward way of thinking. Instead of marriage people should enter into a contract that could be renewed or not, depending on the mutual agreement of both people.

Why, he'd suggest it to her, once he had her back in the sack. But first, he had to get there before that wily Jamie did.

He'd been to a bash at Jamie's some time ago, and remembered how to get there. Hopefully recognize the house. He lived with a couple of other guys, also snow boarders, and they had a big party house on a lake at the end of the street. It was about a mile out of town, and although he couldn't remember where to turn off, he followed his instincts.

There it was. The lights were on, and Jamie's new black Ram truck was parked in the driveway. He breathed a sigh of relief when he didn't see Tara's Mini. He did a slow drive by then hit the highway again, heading straight to Tara's place.

Her car was in the carport, and without further thought he parked behind her and knocked on the side door. He probably should have called first. Somebody knocking on her door at this time of night deserved a 911 call.

"Who is it?" she asked in a fearful voice, and had the good sense not to open the door.

"It's me. Dev."

"What are you doing here?" Now instead of fear, her voice was laced with a healthy dose of anger.

"If you open up, you'll find out."

"No. Go away. I have a right to be mad at you."

"You do, and that's why I'm here." He knew he sounded like a real first class wimp, but that didn't stop him. "Please? Come on, babydoll. I need to explain."

"Explain what? That you have every right to date whoever you want? I know that. I agree. You do." She sniffed. "So why aren't you doing it?"

There was silence for a second while he tried to gather his thoughts and think of something really compelling to say. The contract idea would probably not be a big seller right now.

"I don't want to be with Marissa. I want to be with you." Honesty was sometimes the best policy. And hopefully, it was also the exact words she wanted to hear.

"I agreed to your seeing other women, but I don't like it," she added softly.

"I know. I'm sorry. Will you let me in? Please? I want to see you."

"Why?" Her tone turned icy cool. "You're missing your big chance with that model girl."

"She's nice, but I like you better." He put his head against the door and waited. She might be angry but at least she wasn't sobbing. He had a hard time dealing with a woman's tears.

"You're just saying that, because she'll be leaving, and I'll be staying."

"No, that's not true." Okay, it might be a little true, but losing Tara was enough to put a scare in him. It was worse than having that love bug thing. "I realized something tonight. I didn't want you with anyone else either. So, that's why I'm here."

"Really?" she said in a small voice.

"Yes really. Come on, it's cold out here. Won't you please let me in? Then you can tell me what a jerk I am, and give it to me face to face."

He heard the door being unlocked, and then she peeked out. It looked like she'd been crying. "You can come in, but not for long. I'm tired and I want to go to bed."

"Thanks. I won't keep you."

She stepped back and he walked in, locking the door behind him.

He didn't kiss her, although he wanted to. Instead he walked into the living room and sat down on the sofa. She followed and took a seat across from him.

"Okay." She folded her arms, tucked her legs up under her, and gave him a pouting look. "What did you want to say to me?"

He was tongue-tied suddenly. The whole contract idea didn't seem as logical as it had at first, and besides, just looking at her made his throat dry, his pulse race, and his heart yearn. There was definitely something about her that was getting under his skin, and he needed to tread very carefully before he was pulled under like quicksand.

"I've said most of it already. I didn't want you with Jamie. I didn't want to be with Marissa, either. The moment I saw you, I knew I didn't want her. You blind me to other women. I wish you didn't, but there you have it. Satisfied?"

"Well, you don't have to be so mad about it." She frowned, and then peeked out at him from under her long lashes. "Do I really? Blind you, like that?"

"Yeah. Sucks, doesn't it?" He folded one leg over the other, and picked at the knobby material on the arm rest with his fingers. He felt squirmy all of a sudden. Out of his depth.

"Not really." A hint of a smile crossed her face. "I kind of like it."

"Really?" He looked up and caught her gaze. "How about you? Do you want to be with anyone besides me?"

"No. I don't think so. But still, this is crazy. I've only been here for a couple of weeks. We barely know each other, and it's ridiculous to be exclusive. Isn't it?"

He got up from the sofa and grabbed her hands. "You're too far away from me. I need you closer for this discussion." He led her back to the sofa and she sat next to him. He could feel the warmth of her thigh next to his.

He put an arm around her and drew her head down to his shoulder. He kissed the top of her head. "You feel good."

"So do you," she murmured.

"Do we have to talk anymore tonight?"

"What do you want to do?"

"I want to kiss you for a long time, then I'll leave and let you get some rest."

"You're not going to try any funny business?"

"Not tonight. I think we should let things fall the way they should."

She looked up at him. "I like that. It's a brilliant idea." She raised her chin, offering her mouth. "You can kiss me now."

He kissed her gently, tenderly for a long time, then as her breath quickened their mouths grew hungrier, demanding more. He stroked her back and drove his tongue down her throat as she squirmed against him, and then he was on top of her, fully dressed, their bodies pressing into each other, wanting what their misguided heads wouldn't allow.

Finally, he pushed himself away, and stood up on shaking legs. "I can't do this. I better leave."

"But I want you to stay."

He bent down and kissed her softly. "Not tonight. Let's try to go slow. It won't be easy." He put her hand on his crotch. "This is what you do to me."

"Oh, Dev." He could hear the desperation in her voice and he felt it too.

"Good night, Tara. Lock the door behind me."

She threw a pillow at his back, and grinning, he whistled on the way to his Jeep. It had turned out to be quite a night after all.

CHAPTER TWENTY-TWO

Tara had a restless night. She'd been in love a few times--
or at least thought she was--but this was different. It went
deeper, into a more primitive level, where she felt urges
she'd never had before. One moment she was riding high,
like being on an angel's wing floating in a dreamy cloud.
Then the next moment reality dumped her ass on the
ground and made her wise up. Devon was a player. He
had no desire to fall in love and have the responsibility of
a family any more than she did. They were like-minded
when it came to that whole marriage package idea. *Forever
and ever, until death do you part—oh, my gosh, just kill me now.*

Yet, he had turned down a huge opportunity to get laid
with one of the most gorgeous women Tara had ever
seen. That had to say something, right? Why would he do
that for her? She didn't promise him anything, and they'd
only known each other a few weeks. The mountains were
his world, but this was only a pit stop for her. She'd
always imagined herself near the beach, so California had
naturally appealed to her. But no way could she imagine
mountain living as a permanent existence.

Oh, but Devon. What was it about him that made her heart sing and bring alive hopes and dreams that had barely existed? Well, whatever it was, she needed to get rid of it, because she really, really didn't want to be trapped. Not here in this small mountain village, not when so many places beckoned to her at once.

Her stomach jumped with nerves, like she had a nest of grasshoppers living in there.

Unable to sleep, she finally got out of bed and decided to bake some healthy muffins. She'd box them up for Devon and Kyle, sure they'd appreciate some home baked goods. Heck, she might try out some new recipes too. She got a large pan out, two different flours, baking powder and soda, oat bran, cooking oats, wheat germ, sugar, blueberries, walnuts, banana, buttermilk and eggs.

When the counter was crowded with delicious ingredients she measured each and added them to a large bowl and gently stirred, folding in the blueberries and walnuts at the end. She hummed as she worked. As always the baking soothed her.

Once everything was done, and the batter in the pans, she popped them in the oven and made a half pot of coffee. She sat down in her favorite chair to wait for the muffins, and gazed out at the snow covered mountain. It was pleasant here, and Devon was certainly an exciting diversion, but she must exercise caution and not forget about her long term goals. Gotta keep the eye on the prize, she told herself.

This was not her final stop, and she didn't want to get too comfortable and relinquish a fantastic opportunity to move forward with her career. It was what she had worked so hard for, and relationships would only hold her back and end up breaking her heart. People didn't stay around forever, and she preferred to be the one to leave.

She felt a pang in her chest, just thinking about leaving Devon behind. It wouldn't be easy, but she could do it, and knowing him, he might even help her pack her bags. After all, she'd only come here for the winter, one year at the most. Then she'd move along, find a place with a beach to call home.

Besides, he didn't want to get hooked up any more than she did. He'd left tonight when he could have stayed. And he hadn't answered her when she'd suggested that it might be too soon for them to be faithful. What did that mean? He didn't want to be?

Damn, he was an irritating man. Forced his way in and then didn't take her to bed. So, if he didn't want her just for sex, what the heck did he want from her? Hell, it was too confusing and she was getting a headache.

She took the muffins out of the oven, set them on the counter to cool, and went back upstairs to catch another hour of sleep.

When she woke, the birds were chirping, the sun streaming through the windows, and the smell of fresh baked muffins teased her nose and made her mouth water. She threw on a robe, and went downstairs to make another pot of coffee. Idly, she buttered a muffin, broke it in half, and popped it in her mouth without thinking. She hadn't eaten a muffin in years. She let the sweet taste linger on her tongue, and swallowed it almost with regret.

Not willing to wait for the coffee, she took several more bites, finishing the first muffin and reaching for a second.

It wasn't a sweet, she told herself. It had all healthy ingredients and was made from rolled oats. She closed her eyes remembering how she and her mother had enjoyed baking together, making cookies or brownies or cupcakes. They'd talk about everything and nothing as they licked the frosting off their fingers, then sit and drink tea or milk and eat their specially created desserts. After her mother's passing, she'd lost her taste for sweets. Until now.

She imagined herself sharing moments like that with Devon. Sitting at her counter talking for hours, baking together, exchanging kisses. It could happen if she let it. She held the trump card, if she was willing to take a chance. Her pulse raced and she felt almost giddy. Whatever fears were holding her back from a loving relationship could be resolved. If she let it happen.

She stood up suddenly, flying into motion. She checked her cupboards and supplies in her fridge, realizing that yes, she had all the ingredients to bake a cake. A two layered chocolate, hazelnut torte that the two of them would enjoy after work. Like she had with her mother.

She knew she was floating on that cloud again, the one that defied reality, but baking always elevated her mood. Perhaps she could finally put her mother's sad memories to rest and only remember the happier ones. When the cake was done, she took it out of the oven and let it cool while she showered and dressed for work. Then she wrapped up the rest of the muffins and left the cake in the pan, taking both with her. The car would be like an icebox, so she needn't worry about leaving it for hours.

She arrived at the Cascade Resort early, eager to get the day started so she could spend a few hours with the man she loved. Or didn't love. Whatever. He certainly had her doing cartwheels, one way or another.

Once she had her chef's hat on, she decided she'd played by the book long enough and now it was time to stir the pot. There were a few small conferences going on, but not anything major to worry about so perhaps Philippe might cut her some slack. She was in a mood to be creative and to hell with ordinary.

Everyone in the kitchen got involved—pans sizzled, pots simmered, and enticing spices and scents filled the air. Tara played her favorite opera and the notes soared over the clamor in the kitchen. It was a glorious day.

"What the hell is going on here?" Philippe said, turning off the music with a flick of his finger.

"What does it look like?" Tara answered with a smile. "Genius at work."

"Well, please work a little quieter," he snapped. "We can hear the damn music in the dining room and down the hall."

"Lovely, isn't it?"

He frowned. "Why do you have to antagonize me every minute of every day?"

"I didn't know that I did," Tara answered brightly. "Perhaps you need a valium?"

Philippe opened his mouth to retort, then closed it again, and whirled about, hands flying in the air and clucking like a pigeon. He fled the room, probably to report her attitude to Marc, but really, what was there to report? Her assistants were happy, and they loved the extra work she heaped on them. She knew that under her guidance, they would be better than they were before. And they shouldn't be afraid to show it. Anyone could be mediocre, but wasn't it better to strive for excellence?

She watched the sly smiles of the assistants at Philippe's retreat, and realized they had as little respect for him as she did.

She clapped her hands. "Okay everyone. Back to work. No opera I'm afraid, but if you want to hum, please go right ahead."

The day flew by, and Tara was exhausted and happy when she left the Cascade to bring her hand made treats to her two favorite men. She called Devon's cell to check if he was home or working, but he didn't pick up. It was only four, and the bar didn't get busy for another hour or so. They staggered their opening and closing she knew, and someone could still be home which would save her from delivering her home baked goods to the bar. Besides, she'd never been to his cabin and had a sudden curiosity to see the place.

She found his address easy enough, and discovered it was only half a dozen blocks away. It wasn't like she was snooping, after all she had a gift to bring. Within five minutes she was pulling up his driveway, wondering who owned the Mercedes.

It didn't take her long to find out.

The gorgeous model Devon had been chatting in the bar came out of the house, just as Tara was deliberating whether or not she should go in or back up. Too late.

Marissa's body shielded the person she so desperately wanted to see, but by now Tara's internal alarm system was shrieking wildly, warning her of the danger of heartbreak.

Her stomach clenched, and prickles of uncertainty made her skin itch. She backed out quickly, fearing the worst. She wanted to go home and bury her head in the pillows, afraid of being hurt once again. No one had ever loved her enough to stay around for the long haul. Everyone left her, even her own mother.

Nothing could protect her from learning the truth. She needed to know who was working and who was at the cabin in the afternoon with the voluptuous model-turned-designer from Milan.

She pulled up in front of the Cock & Bull, hopped out, and slammed the door behind her. Her heart sank when she saw the man standing behind the bar.

"Hi, Tara." Kyle stopped checking his liquor supplies, and put his two hands on the counter. He gave her a friendly smile. "Devon should be in soon. He called to say something had come up."

"Something came up all right." She batted back tears, sucked in a breath, and kept her chin high. "He's at home with that Italian woman. So we both know what happened."

"No way." Kyle shook his head. "He's into you. Not her."

"I think he was into her, just a few minutes ago." She knew she was close to a crying jag. No way would she let Devon or his younger brother see how much his tomcatting around bothered her. "You can tell him not to call me anymore."

She swept out the door, head high, shoulders back. When she got into her car, her shoulders sagged, and tears spilled down her cheeks.

Oh, what a convincing liar he was! Telling her he didn't want to be with anyone else, that he wanted to be exclusive. Right! He was probably laughing at her right now, thinking how gullible she was.

Well, she'd show him. If he wanted to do every damn woman in the village and the surrounding cities, that was fine by her.

She didn't need him. She didn't need anybody.

CHAPTER TWENTY-THREE

Devon had just wolfed down a sandwich and was getting ready to head off to work when the knock came at the door. Since few people ever dropped by out of the blue, Tara came to mind. Maybe she'd decided to pay him a visit. Last night he'd left her appetite unsatisfied, that much he knew.

He didn't mind being a few minutes late--not for a chance to pleasure her. "Tara," he said, opening the door and wearing a welcoming grin.

"Wrong girl. Hope you don't mind."

Marissa. What was she doing here?

"Hey. Hi." He forced another smile, but he wasn't ready to deal with her right now. Whatever she wanted, was probably something she couldn't have. Obviously, she'd looked up his home address, which alone made him cautious. She could be a serial stalker for all he knew. They'd never been on a date, and had only skied together once. What the hell was she bothering him for? He'd had his share of pushy woman, and it turned his stomach sour.

She raised a perfectly arched brow. "Mind if I come in?"

He did mind, but good manners didn't allow him to slam the door in her face. "Sure you can, but only for a minute." He opened the door to let her through.

She smiled as she brushed past. "Don't look so scared. I'm not going to bite."

He gave a fake laugh, although she had touched on his fear. "I'm actually on my way to work. You could follow me to the bar if you like." That was a good idea. Much safer there. He had a mental image of being in a small fish bowl, circled by a gorgeous, dangerous piranha.

"Perhaps later. But I wanted to catch you before you left." She trailed her fingers up his chest. "You ran out on me last night. I thought we'd arranged to get together?"

"I'm sorry about that, but there was something important I had to do."

"Maybe a cute pastry chef?"

He sighed, and ran a hand over his face. Guilt wasn't pretty. "Look, Marissa. I admit I went over there. You saw her at the bar. She was really upset with me and I realized I didn't want to lose her."

"I see. Well, I'd hate to come between the two of you, and I won't." She gave a seductive smile. "I'm leaving tomorrow. Long gone, out of your hair." She tossed her head back and laughed. "I would hate to see you have any regrets, so why don't you and I take advantage of this moment?" Her eyes narrowed, reminding him again of that deadly fish. "You could give me a wonderful sendoff."

She had taken two steps forward, effectively backing him against the wall. She smelled like an expensive perfume. Not flowery, just subtle. Classy. She was close enough that her large breasts lightly brushed his chest. He swallowed hard. His dick was starting to act up, encouraging him to agree to her wishes. He gritted his teeth, and told his manly self to obey, and stop trying to get him in trouble.

He might hate himself in the morning, but he had no choice. Not if he wanted to spend more time with Tara. Hadn't they agreed just last night to take this one day at a time? It wasn't even twenty-four hours. He couldn't do this to her—not for a woman who meant nothing at all.

He took Marissa's arms and pushed her away. "Can't do that. I've decided to see how things work out with Tara. I haven't had a steady girlfriend for quite a few years, not sure if I can handle it or not. But that's the deal."

Marissa's blood red lips tilted at the corners. "You could always wait until tomorrow to start this relationship, couldn't you? Don't have to do it right this very second." She grabbed his crotch. "See. I know you want to."

He pushed her hand away. "You are heartless. Brutal, in fact. Normally, I'd like that." He brushed her aside. "Unfortunately your timing is off."

"I don't usually ask twice." Her eyes were like daggers as they scanned his face.

He walked to the door and opened it. "Sorry."

"I'm sure you are." She shrugged, and sashayed toward him, pasting a smile on her face. "You'll never know what you're missing." At the doorway, she leaned in and gave him a full bodied kiss. He sometimes thought of kisses like wine. Pinot—too light, Riesling—too sweet, but a full bodied Cabernet could be just right.

He accepted the kiss, but he didn't exactly kiss her back. Well, maybe only a little, but his heart wasn't in it.

She turned and left, and he waited until her car rounded the corner, before locking the door behind him. He left through the garage, and thought about her and Tara as he drove to work. Both women were beautiful, strong, enticing, but Tara had a softness and a sweetness that Marissa lacked.

When he walked into the bar Kyle gave him a funny look. "You're a little late. Anything you want to tell me?"

"No. Just got held up." Devon stepped behind the bar, hung up his jacket, and glanced around at the hundred bottles of liquor reflected by a mirror, and did a mental inventory.

"Held up? That could be interesting," Kyle said, with a quirky smile on his face. "You see Marissa by chance?"

"Matter of fact, I did." Devon frowned. "She stopped by for a few minutes. How did you know?"

"I have spies everywhere. So, just a few minutes?" Kyle chuckled and gave him a skeptical look. "That's all the time you took? Hell, man. Thought you were better than that."

"What are you going on about?" He glanced at his brother as anger boiled inside.

"Tara was here. Said she popped over to your place and saw you with Marissa. She figured you did her, and I'm guessing you did too."

"You're nuts, and she's wrong. I told Tara last night that I'd be straight with her." Heat rose up his collar. He didn't want to admit this to his brother, who'd mock him for sure. "Said we'd see how things work out."

"Whatever you thought might happen between you two hasn't a hope in hell now. Way I see it, you might want to take a second shot at Marissa."

"Stop the bullshit. You're the one who's been saying I should be planning a wedding." His gut tightened. "Why the sudden change of heart?"

"You blew it, man. Tara looked heart broken. Now you're going to grow old, alone and cynical. Probably only get one chance at that happily-ever-after."

"Go to hell."

"Naw. This place is a lot more fun," Kyle answered and smirked.

Devon lifted a fist, ready to smash something, preferably Kyle's know-it-all-smile. Wanted to knock it as far as Serendipity and back. "Give it a rest. I'm up to my ears with this stuff. Women, the bar, you! Just need to get laid once in a while, and that's it. No bigger aspirations than that."

"You're a sad old man."

"Stop saying that, or I swear, we'll do battle right here and now."

"Watch that Irish temper, Dev. It could get the better of you."

"Why don't you fuck off? Go," he shouted. "Take the night off. Go see Lisa. Or Marissa for that matter. Just get out of my sight."

Kyle laughed. "Jeez, Dev. I didn't know you cared."

That was it. He raised his hand and was getting ready to ram it down Kyle's throat, when a group of young skiers entered the bar. They were loud and obnoxious, and ready to drink hearty. He put his fist down and went to work, although he still simmered inside. He'd never been so close to rearranging Kyle's face before. Sure they'd rough housed growing up, and probably exchanged a punch or two. Sibling stuff. But this had been different. Personal. He didn't like it.

Within the hour the bar was packed, and Devon was too busy to think about Tara or his brother. It gave him a chance to cool down and get his head on straight. His real anger was aimed at himself. He didn't particularly like the person he'd become.

They closed the bar around eleven, and Devon drove over to Tara's. He sat in the car for a while, debating whether he should knock on the door. He couldn't see any lights on and if she were sleeping he'd sure hate to wake her. And yet, he'd feel like a real heel if she was crying over him.

Broken hearted, huh? Damn, he didn't like it when he disappointed people. Like Ken's young sister, Christy. She'd been a nice girl, but he hadn't been interested. He should have made that clear, but he hadn't and then she'd been hurt. Well, things would be different with Tara. He would do the right thing by her.

They had a connection, something drawing them together, whether ready or not.

CHAPTER TWENTY-FOUR

Once Tara got home, she'd cried for a good half hour, sobbing like her heart had truly been broken, not just bruised by another uncaring guy. When her sobs resided, she got up, washed her face, and warmed up some lentil soup.

Now, an hour later, she was sipping on good red wine, sitting at her computer checking out available positions on the Grande Cascade website. By spring, she wanted to be far away from here. Someplace hot, tropical, with plenty of palm trees and cabana boys.

Let Devon freeze his ass off here, playing games with his city girls. She would not stay to watch or to care. There was a whole big world waiting for her, and she for it. Sipping her wine, she settled back in her chair, willing to admit that at this precise moment there was nowhere to go. The only pastry chef opening was in Phoenix. Granted it was hot and had palm trees, but it was also very dry, scorching hot in the summer and had no freakin' beach.

Well, not to worry, she had a few more months before she could pull up roots. Roots—that was almost funny.

She was as rootless as they came, more like a leaf that blows with the wind until it finds a place to settle.

She wiped a tear from her eye. She could like it here. The clean smell of the cool fresh air, the sight of the snowcapped mountains, the evergreen forests and the plentiful lakes and streams. So different from living in the big cities which she'd expected to make her happy. But she hadn't found her happiness there. The closest she'd come to that emotion was the time she'd spent in Devon's company. It wasn't all sex. She enjoyed their teasing remarks, the light flirtation, the way his eyes would warm as he looked at her. Some things you couldn't fake, and his affection for her was real.

Unfortunately, he also had affection for other women, and she'd thought it wouldn't bother her, but it did. That was why she needed to get out of dodge while the getting was good. If she stayed, her feelings would only grow deeper.

The thought of leaving Devon gave her a sharp pang. Sadly, she missed him already and she hadn't even left yet.

She took another long sip from her glass. What if she stayed and fought for her man? Marissa would be leaving in a day or two, and he'd said he wanted to give their relationship a try. Yeah, right! Lying bastard. His effort had only lasted what? Less than a day? No, Marissa could have him, or some other poor sucker, because no way in hell did she want a conniving, lying, two-timing bastard sleeping in her bed, working his way into her heart.

She'd already had a few of those in her lifetime. Why did she always fall for the bad guys? Why couldn't she love a sincere, nice man who wanted commitment and a family? It had to be a failing on her part. Something missing inside of her. But she knew the answer to that question, had always known. She fell for the exact type she needed—the kind that didn't want her. That way she could leave anytime she wanted. She wouldn't be trapped.

Admitting this was her problem to finding happiness was one thing. Finding a solution was another. She didn't want to be doomed to a life of loneliness, but she couldn't see her way out of it.

She jolted. What was that noise? Something landed on her window with a thud. Looked like snow. What the heck?

She got up out of her seat, and peered outside. A patch of snow slid down the window and she was still looking out, when another splat hit it again. Who the hell was throwing snowballs at her house? Some neighborhood kids?

She grabbed her coat, put on her boots and opened the front door. "Who's out there?"

Devon appeared from the side of the house, hands in pockets, looking sheepish. "It's me. I didn't see any lights on so I didn't want to knock on your door. I walked around the house and saw your reading lamp from the back window."

"So you decided to throw snowballs at me?"

He grinned, bent over, picked up one, and tossed it right at her. "Yeah. Why not? You're outside now. Fair game." He picked up another batch of snow and creamed her with it.

Of all the nerve! What the heck was he up to? He expected to have sex with Marissa in the afternoon, and then come by her place at night, laughing and teasing her to come out and play.

Well, she'd just see about that! She picked up some snow with her bare hands, packed it as hard as she could and when he took several steps in her direction she let him have it. Got him right in the nose.

He sputtered as the snow melted on his face, but he kept on coming. Quickly, she picked up another patch of snow next to her feet, and threw it at his head. Now his hair was wet too. She watched it slide down his collar, and grinned in triumph. Oh, he so deserved this. He wasn't even defending himself, so he knew he had it coming.

That infuriated her even more. She was about to pick up another ball when he took two giants steps forward, and grabbed her arms.

"Okay, you've had your revenge. Want to really get into it out here, or should we go in and talk?"

"Talk? I have nothing to say to you! Well, maybe I do. You're a low down dirty rat, and I should have kept well away from you. Had enough warnings, didn't I?" Tears sprang to her eyes. "Heck. You told me so yourself."

"You knew better, but got involved with me anyway." He lifted a finger and wiped her tear away. "And I with you. We didn't want this, but we got it, dammit to hell." He pulled her into his arms. "I can't stay away from you."

With those simple words the fight went out of her.

"What about Marissa? I saw you with her today. I'd come over to give you something—some muffins and a cake I made for you and Kyle. And she was just leaving. I saw you kiss."

"That was all there was to it. She was hoping for more, but I told her that I'd made a decision about you."

"Well, I don't want your decision. You should have had your fun." Her teary eyes lifted to his. "What are you doing here, anyway? What decision?"

"If you'd stop talking so much, I'd show you." He pulled her head toward him, settled his mouth on hers, and sucked any more words, any breath, right out of her.

She wobbled toward him, and he gathered her in his arms, holding her tight.

"Can we go in now?" He whispered in her ear.

"Okay." She took his hand and led him inside.

They dropped their coats on the floor, took off their boots, and turned to each other. She grabbed his sweater and pulled it over his head. It fell on the floor next to his jacket.

Her sweater followed next. She pulled at his belt buckle, got the thing undone, zipper too. She pulled his jeans down and they fell to his ankles, jockey shorts and all. With her ice cold hands, she cupped him. "You're a bastard, but I want you."

He grinned, and unzipped her jeans too. Pushed them over her fanny, and pulled her in tight. "Come to me, baby. I'll make everything all right."

They both kicked out of their jeans, and he picked her up and carried her fireman style up the stairs and tossed her on the bed. Then he jumped down beside her, and rolled her over on top of him. He kissed and stroked her for a long time, until the heat between them became unbearable. She mounted him and he slid inside.

Using her arms, she arched her back so she could look at his face as they made love. She wanted to see every expression, and know if he was faking this or not.

His eyes were open and on her. "I'm sorry I made you cry." His hands played with her nipples, turning her on so much she could only rub against him, wanting more. More hands, more of him filling her inside and out. More softly spoken words, more deep sighs, more deep thrusts. She wanted his all.

She moved against him, breathing heavily, rocking, rocking, letting the rhythm of their mating build in anticipation, knowing that the closer she came to release, the deeper he was slipping into her heart, her soul. She should fight this, but the sensations were too much, too intense, too wonderful to end. He pushed one more time, and she took him deeply, her back still arched, her skin slippery with sweat, theirs bodies slapping together, hearts beating wildly as they began to peak.

Tara couldn't stand another second, and cried out his name as her first release came. A second later, he bellowed and shook, joining her in a wild orgasm that rocked both their worlds. They held on tight as first one orgasm shook her, quickly followed by another. Each began to peter out, then started up again, and she was crying and laughing, and couldn't quite stop.

Finally, she pushed away. "Enough. Dear God! How many was that?"

He laughed, and nibbled on her shoulder. "You expect me to keep count?"

"No. It's just never happened to me before. I feel so weak, so depleted, and yet so full." She found his mouth and kissed him softly. "Thank you."

"For what?" he asked tenderly, tucking a lock of hair behind her ear.

"For saving this for me. I'm so glad you didn't sleep with Marissa."

"Marissa who?" he said, his eyes lighting with a smile. "I only want you. Now can I tuck you in, and sleep here tonight?"

"I wish you would."

He wrapped his arms around her and curled up into her back. He dropped a few kisses on her shoulders, behind her ears, and cupped her breasts. Before long, she heard his even breathing and knew he'd fallen asleep. She laid awake thinking of how fast he'd woven his way into her heart, and how it would hurt to leave him, but leave him she would. This was Devon's home, but not hers. She yearned for new adventures and fresh challenges, and didn't allow anything to get stale.

Mammoth was no different, and not even a man like Devon could keep her here.

CUPID

Together at last, I thought, and sighed with real pleasure. It looks as if these two lovebirds have stopped their squawking and will embrace this new found love of theirs. I've never had a couple seem more compatible than these two here. Without a doubt I'm sure that Devon loves her very much, and Tara has only to open her eyes to see it. That poor child has never been happy since her mother passed away. Many times I've heard her weeping at night, calling out for her mother in her troubled sleep.

It makes my heart sore, but seeing her now with a half-smile on that pretty face of hers as she cuddles into Devon's strong arms, well, it eases the weight I carry around when I know my special ones are not happy.

The snow fight was inspirational! Planting that thought into Devon's head was a stroke of genius. And Tara had quickly joined in the fun. The fight had allowed them both to let off steam, and to get them sexually aroused, I do think. Still I shouldn't preen so much, but I can't refrain as I congratulate myself. I am quite sure that I deserve a reward for tonight's success, and I already have one in mind.

I hop down from my perch near the window and slip downstairs, eager to sneak a bite of that dark almond chocolate that I'd spotted earlier in the cupboard. I break off a tiny piece and take it with me to Tara's favorite chair next to the window. I sit with my legs tucked under me, munching on the delicious chocolate and watch the silent pure white fluffs of snow as they fall from the sky. The snow brightens the night with magic and covers the ground like sugar-dust, bringing a sense of peace.

If all goes well, then my job here will be done and I'll soon return to Serendipity Falls and find other lonely people to unite.

A guilty thought flashed through my mind. Why did I ever complain about my lot in life when I have the most wonderful, satisfying job of all? Tears of shame fill my eyes and yet my heart is full. Love is the greatest gift I can bring the world, and to be a Cupid is simply next to divine.

CHAPTER TWENTY-FIVE

Tara awakened slowly as if from a long, deep sleep. Twitching, she attempted to move but found herself trapped. The blankets were wrapped around her feet, and someone's arms prevented her from escape. She tried to twist out of his grasp. Who was holding her? Where was she?

She heard a soft moan of protest, and stopped struggling. It was Devon. She remembered now, and breathed in a deep sigh of relief. Her memory flashed back to the snow fight, the love making, the things they said to each other. And the words they didn't.

Moving ever so gently, she disentangled herself from his arms, not wanting him to see her this way. Her body was in a cold sweat, and she'd awakened terrified and shaking. Not the first time, or likely the last. Disturbing dreams were nothing new.

Tonight, she'd been running, running in a forest and someone had been after her. She heard his feet pounding right behind her, gaining on her, and then his arms had captured her and thrown her to the ground. His big body had covered hers, and she'd been trapped like a bird in a cage, desperate to flee.

She'd heard her mother's voice calling her, and that had sent her scurrying into the forest. But the harder and longer she ran, the farther the voice moved away. As much as she loved her mother, she wished the haunted dreams would stop so she could sleep in peace. They didn't bring her closer, but left her weak, frightened, desolate and alone.

Carefully, she shifted her bottom toward the side of the bed so she could slip out, undetected. Devon stirred, and flung his arm out as if searching for her. She held her breath and tip-toed into the bathroom, closing the door silently behind her. She glanced in the mirror and saw her wide, anguished eyes, her flushed face, and the perspiration coating her skin.

She turned on the shower, waited for it to turn warm before stepping in. She washed her hair, and cleansed her body, letting the steady flow of water wash away the lingering fears and secure her in the present.

This had happened before--when she got close to somebody she'd have heart palpitations, nightmares, and dreams of flight. Panic attacks, where she couldn't breathe until she was alone. One of the things that kept her running.

She dried herself with a big, fluffy towel, and slipped into a robe. When she came out of the bathroom Devon was sitting up, arms stretched behind his head. His dark hair was tousled, eyes still heavy from sleep, and the cleft in his chin begged to be touch.

"You showered already?" he mumbled with a smile. "You should have called me to wash your back."

Needing his warmth and his touch, she stepped over to him. Smiling, she brushed the hair out of his eyes, touched the cleft in his chin, and dropped a kiss on his lips. "You were sleeping so sound. I hoped I wouldn't wake you."

He wrapped his arms around her and pulled her down next to him. Kissed the top of her head. "I had a nice time last night. Thought we might be able to have a repeat performance."

She tilted her head to look at him. "You mean the snow fight?"

"I mean me and you in bed, having a hellova good time."

"Figured that's what you meant." She laced her fingers into his thick chest hair. "But don't you have to go to work, or ski or something?"

"Not 'til later. I have plenty of time to do some things I forgot about last night."

"Oh, yeah? Like what things?"

He flipped over and undid the belt on her robe. "I forgot to kiss you here." His mouth roamed over her stomach, tickling her, and then he licked her breasts. His teeth gently pulled at her nipples while his hand slid lower. "And to kiss you here."

"Devon. Don't do that. Remember I'm a one dimensional girl."

"Not any more you're not." And with that he got down to business and proved it.

After another amazing lesson in love, Devon picked her up and took her back to shower, and she washed him down as he did her. Eventually, they managed to keep their hands off each other long enough to dress and put the coffee on.

Tara got to work, making crisp bacon and a cheese and mushroom omelet with whole grain toast. Devon sipped on his coffee and watched the morning news on TV. The birds were chirping and there was another foot of fresh snow. It was a beautiful morning and a sparkling start of a new day.

She remembered her nightmare, and tried to push it out of her mind. Not again. She had no wish to run. She was just settling in, had found a wonderful guy, a great job, and life was good. So go away Mother, go away bad dreams, and let me be happy, she said silently, watching him with tears prickling the back of her eyes.

This man could bring her joy. If only she could let him.

They ate their breakfast, finished two cups of coffee, and then she pushed him out the door. "Go ski. I know you want to, and I have to work again in a few hours."

He gave her a kiss. "I might just do that. See you after work?"

"Sounds good. Enjoy the snow."

"Always." She watched him take an ice scraper from his car to clear his windows, while the car warmed up. Although the air was frigid, she waited until he backed down the driveway, hooted his horn, and waved good-bye.

Once inside, she quickly rinsed and put the dishes away, and tided up the kitchen counter. She checked her cell phone and saw her dad had left three messages. She hadn't spoken to him in more than a month and guilt weighed in. He didn't even know that she'd left L.A. and was living in the mountains.

She returned his call, knowing it was three hours later in Florida, nearly noon.

"Tara," his warm voice answered. "Thanks for calling me back. I called your office in L.A. and they said you'd left."

"I'm sorry, Dad. I should have told you sooner, but it happened quickly and then with the packing and everything, I just forgot." She knew it was a piss poor excuse, but it was all that she had to offer. "Anyway, I'm working now in Mammoth, a ski resort not far from San Francisco. I'm still an executive pastry chef with Cascade Resorts. Not much has changed except my location."

"Well, well, well. You certainly do get around, don't you?" He chuckled. "Anyway, I'm sure you're enjoying yourself. The mountains must be nice, huh? All that clean, fresh air. You still ski?"

"A little. When I have time."

"You meet anyone yet? It's high time you found a nice guy and got married."

"I'm still working on my career first, Dad. But I'm seeing someone. I think you'd like him."

"I'm sure I would."

Tara heard him whisper, probably to his wife, "She's met someone." Then he asked, "So, this young man of yours--what does he do?"

"He runs a bar with his brother. They own their own business, and work hard. Devon's also on the ski patrol. He's a good guy, Dad."

"Well, I'm glad. If he's good to you that's all that matters. Must admit though, I figured you'd end up with some ad executive or high powered lawyer type."

"Who knows?" she answered, quick to set the record straight. "I'm not marrying anyone right now. You know me. I like this guy, but I don't stick around long enough to fall in love."

"One day you will." He cleared his throat. "Anyway, the reason I was calling is to say that Laura's daughter just had a baby girl, and she'll be staying with her for a week or two to help out." He hesitated for a second, then blurted, "You haven't visited in a while, and I thought it might be a good chance for us to catch up."

"That's nice, Dad. Congratulate Laura for me."

"Tara, I'd like you to meet Laura and her family. It's time." His voice only carried a hint of reproach. "Any chance you can make it?"

"It's not likely on such short notice." She remembered her dream, her feelings of being trapped, and wondered if that dream was telling her something.

Her stomach churned as her anxiety grew. She hated feeling anxious, confused, like a deer caught in headlights. She was stronger than that. Strong enough to take over the household chores and take care of a dying mother. Strong enough to hold things together when her father closed himself off, and refused to come out of his room for weeks on end. She had been strong once—where had that girl gone?

"I don't know what to say to you, to make things right anymore. Your mom died a long time ago. You're a woman now, not a child." She started to interrupt but he spoke over her. "Keeping yourself at a distance has been hurtful to me and to them. Please, come for a visit," her father's voice broke, "it's high time you did."

That speech had probably been longer than any they'd shared in the past decade. Obviously, it had been on his chest for a while.

She bit her bottom lip, knowing that the rift between them was entirely her fault. "I know, Dad. You're right." She swallowed a lump in her throat. "Maybe I can swing it somehow."

"That would be wonderful. Do try."

She'd been estranged from her father long enough, and refusing to meet his new wife had been childish and insulting behavior. She needed to repair the bridge that separated them. It wasn't flight. She wasn't running from something. It was merely a step in the right direction.

"Let me know today if possible." Her father sounded surprised but pleased. "I can pick you up at the airport, and you can spend a weekend here. Laura's daughter only lives twenty minutes away so we can visit. You're going to like her, sweetheart, and she's going to love you too."

"Sounds good. I miss you, Dad." As an afterthought, she added, "I dreamt of Mom again last night. Those dreams are so disturbing—like she's calling out to me."

"I'm sorry. You two were very close." He cleared his throat. "What you need is a family of your own. Stop moving about so much, and put down some roots."

"I might do that. One day." She laughed. "Okay, I have to make the arrangements but I'm really going to try to be there this weekend. I promise."

They said their goodbyes, and Tara felt positive about her decision. She would spend the weekend getting to know her father's new family, and the distance might shed some clarity on her feelings for Devon without her over-active hormones getting in the way.

CHAPTER TWENTY-SIX

Tara managed to get the weekend off work, claiming a family emergency, which it was in a way. She was the one stuck in a time warp, and blaming him for not grieving forever, was just damn pathetic. Her dad deserved to be happy, and come to think of it, so did she.

Excited about seeing her father, and making amends to Laura for being such a jerk, Tara got to the airport early and had to wait for her flight. She was flying from San Francisco direct to Tampa, a short drive from Sarasota where her dad and Laura lived. Having an hour to kill, she pulled out her E-reader, but her eyes were drawn to the TV monitor. The newscaster had mentioned an avalanche and missing skiers, but she hadn't heard the entire report.

She stood up abruptly, her reader and boarding pass slipped to the ground unnoticed. "Where was the avalanche?" she asked the other passengers gathered around the TV.

"Mammoth. Happened a few hours ago. A ski patroller is missing, and two young kids. Teenagers, I think."

Her knees buckled and she swayed slightly. "Did they give any names?" she asked quickly.

"Not yet. Names haven't been released."

It couldn't be Devon, she assured herself. They had plenty of ski patrollers, and what would be the chances? Next to zero, she decided, dialing his number just the same. They'd talked this morning. He'd probably be on the mountain, ready and eager to assist in a search and rescue.

He didn't pick up, and she left a message for him to call back. Then she called her father and told him she wouldn't be coming. "I'm so sorry, Dad. But I've got to make sure he's safe. Please make my apologies to Laura."

"That's fine, sweetheart. Call me the minute you know."

"I will. I love you."

She only had carry-on baggage and with that in tow, she rushed through the terminal and headed for the parking lot where she'd left her Mini. She called Devon again and when it went to voice-mail, she dialed the number for the bar. No one picked up.

Where was everybody?

It took her a couple of hours to get back to the mountain and she drove right to the village, knowing she'd get answers quicker that way. If Devon was part of the search and rescue team it could be hours before she'd hear back from him.

A large crowd had gathered near the gondola base, obviously waiting for news.

She pressed in close, listening to the hushed voices. People were speaking like they do in a funeral home or a hospital—or when someone is dead. Tingles of fear slid up and wrapped itself around her heart. She'd never had premonitions before, but something was telling her that bad news was coming.

"Who's missing?" she asked no one in general, her eyes sweeping over faces, eager to hear anything but what her heart feared.

"Couple of kids on snowboards, and a ski patroller. There may be more," a young woman answered, then turned back to her male friend.

"Does anyone know who the ski patroller is?" She bit her lip, trying not to sound as panicked as she felt. "Please. I need a name."

"It's the guy who owns the bar," a young, bearded fellow said when no one else spoke. "Not sure of his name. Anyone else know?"

A few people shrugged, and Tara cried out in frustration, "What bar? It's not the Cock & Bull, is it?"

"Yeah, that's the one," the same man answered.

Her heart thumped. "Devon O'Reilley?" she asked, her eyes searching nearby faces. "One of the two brothers?"

"Think so," another guy nodded. "Sounds like the guy, but I don't know for sure."

Tara felt herself sway and someone from behind reached out a hand to steady her. She turned and recognized the young woman's face. "Mila? Oh, Mila. Is it true?"

Blinking back tears, Mila nodded. "Tara, I'm sorry you found out this way. I didn't know how to reach you."

"I was at the airport. Planned to see my family this weekend and heard it on the TV news. Is it Devon? Do they know for sure?"

Mila's face crumpled. "Yes. I'm afraid so. He saved a woman who was skiing with her two teenage sons. Then when he tried to find the boys, he was swept away. That was four hours ago. He has a tracker device and they pretty much know where he is but haven't been able to dig him out. The area is still not stable, and they can't get their equipment in safely."

"Dear God. Are you saying that he'll be buried deeper if they try to rescue him?" Tara shut her eyes and put her hands over her face, thinking of Devon trapped under feet of snow, buried alive. She let out a whimper.

Mila pulled Tara into her arms, and whispered, "They will. As soon as the area is safe they'll get him out. They know where he is. It's just a matter of time." She brushed Tara's hair off her forehead and looked her straight in the eyes. "He'll come back to us. I know he will."

Tara's teeth chattered, and she gave a half laugh, half sob. "He better. I've only just realized how much he means to me."

"Glad to hear it," Mila answered, "since I knew right away."

"Oh, Mila. I knew I was going to like you." She linked arms with Devon's sister. "Where's Kyle? We should stick together."

"Last time I spoke to him he was at the Main Lodge. We agreed to wait at different places in case he was brought to one or the other."

"Let's get out of here and make some kind of plan," Tara suggested.

They navigated a path away from the crowd, heading for the lodge. Once inside, Mila called Kyle and before she had time to say a word, he asked, "Any news?"

"I hoped you might tell me." Mila looked at Tara, and shook her head. "Tara's with me. Can we meet you somewhere?"

"I'm still at the Village. Why don't you both come here?"

"We will. The Village is closer to the hospital, it makes sense they'll take them there."

Tara held Mila's hands in hers, and noticed how cold and clammy they both were. "I'm going to run back to the cabin first and change. I was on my way to Florida, and I'm not dressed for warmth." Wearing only thin slacks and a light weight jacket, she felt the cold and dampness inside and out. She'd been traveling in a pair of shoes, and her toes were like chips of ice. She needed a ski jacket, boots, a hat and gloves for the hours of wait that lay ahead.

"Do that. We don't want you getting sick on top of this." She offered a sad smile. "Meet us at the Village Lodge. I'll call you if we get any news."

"Give me your cell," Tara said, taking it out of her hand. She punched in her number and gave it back. "There. Now you can reach me anywhere, anytime."

Mila blinked rapidly, fighting tears. "Hurry back."

"Of course. Back in less than an hour." She turned, half way to the door. "If you see Dev before I do. Tell him I love him."

Tara got back to the cabin, then ran upstairs and took a long, warm shower, allowing her body to thaw out and her tremors to stop. She dressed quickly in a pair of jeans, a turtle necked sweater, thick socks, and went back downstairs. She made some soup, several sandwiches, then put the soup in a thermos, bagged the sandwiches, and put them in a canvas tote. It might be an all-night vigil for all they knew.

She was all set to go, when suddenly the shudders started again. She was so cold, as cold as she had been at the age of sixteen when she'd watched her mother die.

But Devon was not going to die, she told herself. He was going to be found, any minute now, and she would be right here waiting for him. He might not love her or want her forever but she was not going to leave him. She had run long enough, and had nowhere else to go. This mountain was a part of Devon, and for that reason alone it was now her home.

CHAPTER TWENTY-SEVEN

Tara found Kyle and Mila sitting in lounge chairs near a roaring fire, sipping on cups of hot chocolate. They looked relaxed and comfortable, which Tara knew was a lie. Their hearts were probably even heavier than hers, their fears multiplied.

"Nothing?" she said in way of greeting. Kyle looked glum and Mila just shook her head.

"Good news, though." Mila seemed determined to be optimistic, and tried to sound quite cheery. "The area is stable and they've started digging. Should be any time now."

Kyle snorted. "He could be dead already. They can't even get a signal. Probably buried so fucking deep, they won't find him until spring."

"Don't say that," Tara snapped. "I know you're worried, but he's down there fighting for his life. He wouldn't want us to give up so easily. I'm sure he's not going to."

"What the hell do you know?" Kyle retorted. "You didn't believe in him a few days ago, why are you even here?"

Mila turned to her brother. "Kyle, that's a horrible thing to say. Tara loves Devon and she has every right to be here with us. She's worried sick. And Devon would want her here."

Tara stood there looking at Kyle, frozen by the cruelty of his remark, the bitter hatred in his eyes. She bit her bottom lip but couldn't stem the tears that flowed, running down her cheeks.

"I won't stay here if you don't want me, but I'm not leaving the mountain. Not until he's found." She dumped the backpack on the big square table in front of them. "I brought a thermal of soup and some sandwiches. It could be a long, long night."

She turned to leave, but Kyle put his foot out, blocking her path. "Sit down. I'm an idiot."

There was a chair next to him and she plopped down before he changed his mind. "I know you're only looking out for your brother's best interests. You're just misguided if you don't think I'm one of them."

Mila smiled and reached for her hand. "Welcome to the family, sister."

Tara smiled through her tears. "Not a sister yet, but when Devon gets home, I'll make sure he drinks gallons of that spring water. Just in case the love bug is real." She felt a ping in the back of her neck. "Ouch. What was that?"

"What?" Kyle asked, looking at her strangely.

"Nothing. Just felt a pain in my neck. Sharp, like a needle."

"Well, if you're not in too much pain, how about passing me a sandwich. I haven't eaten since breakfast."

"That's what I thought." She opened the bag and doled out the sandwiches and poured soup into the Styrofoam cups she'd thought to bring. "Are we okay to eat it here?"

"Probably not a good idea generally," Mila said softly, "but tonight people have more on their minds. We're a tight community and everyone in the village is gathered to wait for one of our own. We're all in this together."

While they ate, Kyle explained how the RECCO, an avalanche rescue system worked. "The skier, like Devon for example, has to have a reflector either in his clothes, his helmet, boots, some place that will pick up a signal and echo it back. All our ski patrollers have it in their jackets, and a lot of serious skiers wear them too."

"Does that send off a signal so they can be found?" Tara asked.

"No, they need a beacon to do that. Again, the ski patrollers carry transceivers to help find people, or if they get caught in an avalanche situation as well. When someone is skiing the descent will activate the device and a low-powered beacon signal will emit. In the event of an avalanche they can switch the transceiver from transmit into receive mode, so it has dual purposes."

"So that's the signal they got when Devon first disappeared?" Mila asked.

"Yes. But the mountain has a second system, the RECCO, which is a two-way transmitter. The rescue team on the ground or in a helicopter can use their hand held device and pick up on someone's reflector. It bounces back a directional signal that directs the rescuer straight to the reflector. It's not foolproof, but I've seen it work successfully before."

Tara let it sink it, thinking that with two devices he should have already been found. What was keeping them?

"How many feet of snow can it penetrate?" she wanted to know.

"Not sure, but at least thirty."

"Well then, seems like we have nothing to worry about," Tara said it like a bad joke. "Right?"

Mila and Kyle didn't bother to answer, nor had she expected them too. Keeping their spirits up was all for show. They finished their soup and sandwiches, fuel for whatever lay ahead.

"Can they work at night?" Tara asked.

"I expect so. Should be able to work with lanterns if they have too."

Mila looked at both their faces. "He'll be found way before nightfall. I expect to hear something positive within the next hour."

Kyle stood up and grabbed his ski jacket. "You girls stay here where it's warm. I'm going back outside to see what's going on."

"I'm coming too," Mila said, zipping up her own jacket.

"Don't leave me behind." Tara snagged her belongings, and followed them out. "They should have picked up a signal by now. Maybe they're already on their way down."

Kyle gave a disgusted shake of his head. "The ski patrol will call me the minute they have him. I haven't been out of touch with them for a second since the accident happened."

"I'm sorry. I was just trying to be positive."

"Don't. It's hard enough without your cheerful banter." He marched ahead of them, and Tara felt like she'd been tongue lashed as she watched him go.

"I didn't mean anything," Tara whispered, hurt, to Mila.

"He's just so worried, that's all." Mila linked her arm.

They reached the crowd standing around the gondola station and learned that more skiers were missing, or at least, unaccounted for.

"They picked up a signal about thirty minutes ago," someone told them, "but they haven't reached that person yet."

The sun had set, and the air seemed to have dropped about ten degrees. A wind had picked up, and drifts of snow whirled around them. Mila and Tara huddled together, their backs to the wind as minutes dragged by, each one seeming longer than the other. "What if he isn't found," Tara whispered. "How long can he survive buried in that snow?"

"It depends. Some people have survived for days if they get enough oxygen. That's all he needs—an air pocket."

They fell silent once more, and Tara was nearly jumping out of her skin. The light was fading and with the wind, the swirling snow, she was afraid the rescue might be called off until morning. Between her fear for Devon's safety and that of the others missing, combined with the night chill, she was shivering so badly her teeth were chattering.

"Go on inside," Mila told her. "You're freezing to death."

"I don't want to leave," she said reluctantly.

"Go inside, Tara. Getting frostbite won't make Devon happy. I'll hang with Kyle a little longer, then I'll be in too."

Tara nodded and turned to walk away. She'd only taken a few steps when she heard an excited buzz from behind her. She whirled around.

"They've found some survivors. They're bringing them down," she heard someone shout.

Tara ran back to Mila. "Is it Devon? Did they find him?"

"Kyle's trying to find out. He's on the phone now."

A few minutes later, Kyle turned and grinned. He put a thumb up in the air.

Devon was found. Alive.

Kyle came up and hugged his sister, then reached out a hand and brought her into the circle. They were all crying and clinging to each other, and Tara felt such a powerful connection to them, knowing they were her family now.

"We need to go to the hospital," he told them. "They'll be taking the survivors there."

Tara nodded. "I have my own car. I'll meet you at ER?"

"Right. I don't know how soon they'll let us see him, or if he's conscious. Just that's he alive." His face sobered. "The rescue team's still trying to reach others. They've got a few more signals."

Mila wiped her eyes. "It's gonna be a long night. I feel almost guilty that for us the ordeal is over."

"I'm too happy to feel guilty," Tara said. "I'm just so grateful that he's alive."

They walked back to the parking lot together before going their separate ways.

For them the night had become a little brighter, but she sent up a prayer for the others, hoping they too would be reached before long, and brought home safely.

CHAPTER TWENTY-EIGHT

Tara sat next to Devon's bed, long after Kyle and Mila had left to go home. She linked fingers with him and watched him sleep. He looked so peaceful and so dear to her, that she wished she could crawl under the white sheets, rest her head on his chest, and stay there all night close to his heart.

She'd thought loving someone this much would scare the life out of her, and it almost had, but the idea of losing him was far, far worse. If he wanted to get rid of her, well, then he should never have allowed himself to be carried down that mountain. She intended to stay and nurse him back to health for as long as it took. She planned to hang around him so much that he would just have to get used to it, whether he liked it or not.

She wasn't going anywhere. Mammoth was her home too. She sniffed and wiped away a tear.

"What are you crying for?"

She peeked at him through wet lashes. "You're awake."

"Looks that way. So why are you crying?" His fingers tightened on hers. "You hoping I wouldn't wake up?" His mouth twisted in a smile.

"Of course not!" She pulled her hand free, and then seeing his eyes crinkle up at the corners, her heart shifted inside of her, and she flung herself on his chest, and broke into sobs.

He patted her hair. "Don't cry, baby. I'm okay. I'm here, aren't I?"

"Yes." She lifted her head and looked at him. Tears spilled down her cheeks and landed on his chest. She sniffled and swiped away huge, wet drops. "But I was so afraid. I thought...I thought...you might not come back." She let out a big, ripping sob that probably frightened half the ward.

"Oh, sweetheart. I'm here." He shifted over on the bed. "Come here. Lie with me."

She didn't have to be asked twice.

She kicked off her shoes, and slid on the side of the bed, resting her head on his shoulder, her hand on his chest. "I want to spend the night with you. Can I?"

He kissed the top of her head. "I'll ask the nurse to let you stay. Okay?"

"Okay." She moved a little and kissed his lips. "You still feel so cold."

"You'll warm me up. I'll tell them that I need your body warmth."

"That's a good idea. I'm frozen too. Inside," she said, and moved his hand over her heart. "This part of me is only beginning to thaw."

"Because of me?" he asked gently.

"Unless it's the love bug." She giggled. "Of course it's you. I love you like crazy, and you know what? You're not getting rid of me. I refuse to go even if you want me to."

"Is that right?"

"Yes." Her eyes lifted to his. She looked into their warm chocolate colored depths, trying to see all the way to his soul. Did he love her too? "Is that all right with you?"

His sexy lips curved into a smile. "Does it make any difference? You're staying no matter what." His arm swept around her and pulled her close. "So I might as well stop fighting and just get used to it." He rested his chin on her head. "You know something?"

"What?" She lifted her head to see him better.

He kissed the tip of her nose. "I think I can handle you around 24/7. Not just for a year either."

Her heart hummed with excitement. "How long exactly?"

"I had some time today to think clearly while I was buried in that snow. I thought about you, mostly, and how I don't want to let you slip away. Not now. Not ever. I want you around for a very long time. You ever thought about taking a honeymoon in Hawaii? They've got some beautiful beaches there."

"I never thought about it, no. But then, I'd have to get married first, wouldn't I?"

"I know a place where people get married all the time, and no one ever gets a divorce."

"Really? How lovely." She sighed with bliss. "That's sounds so romantic."

"It's the most romantic place in the world. You and I should take a trip there soon. It's called Serendipity Falls."

Her breath hitched in her throat. Her eyes were glued to his, her mouth invitingly close. "Is that a proposal?"

"You bet your sweet ass it is."

"Then yes." She reached for his face so she could kiss him. "Yes." She kissed his eyelids. "Yes." She kissed both cheeks. "And yes." Her mouth found his, and a flood gate opened. All the love stored up inside her for so many lonely years poured into that one long kiss.

And she knew her heart had found its home at last.

CUPID

I love happy endings, don't you? As Tara and Devon repeat their wedding vows, I'm already perched on the edge of the dessert buffet table. I nibble some lovely chocolate and even taste the champagne that flows better than that gosh darn spring water.

Oh, there I go again. But as I listen to the wedding guests gush on and on about that silly love bug, I wish I could find the so called bug myself and squash it to smithereens. But only you and I know that it doesn't exist.

I'm Cupid, and as long as I'm alive this town will continue to thrive and happiness will abound. Next time you're around, be sure to drop in, you hear?

www.ingramcontent.com/pod-product-compliance
Lightning Source LLC
Chambersburg PA
CBHW060053150626
46556CB00017BA/117